About the Editor

John Dale grew up in Hobart and now lives in Sydney. He has worked in a wide variety of jobs and is currently researching his Doctorate at the University of Technology, Sydney. His first book of stories, *The Blank Page*, was published in 1987 and his most recent novel, *Dark Angel*, was published in 1995 in Australia and the UK.

OUT WEST

Australian Dirt

edited by

JOHN DALE

HarperCollins*Publishers*

This project has been assisted by
the Commonwealth Government
through the Australia Council,
its arts funding and advisory body.

HarperCollins*Publishers*

First published in Australia in 1996
by HarperCollins*Publishers* Pty Limited
ACN 009 913 517
A member of the HarperCollins*Publishers* (Australia) Pty Limited Group

HarperCollins*Publishers*
25 Ryde Road, Pymble, Sydney NSW 2073, Australia
31 View Road, Glenfield, Auckland 10, New Zealand
77–85 Fulham Palace Road, London W6 8JB, United Kingdom
Hazelton Lanes, 55 Avenue Road, Suite 2900, Toronto, Ontario M5R 3L2
and 1995 Markham Road, Scarborough, Ontario M1B 5M8, Canada
10 East 53rd Street, New York NY 10032, USA

National Library of Australia Cataloguing-in-publication data:

Out west.
   ISBN 0 7322 5165 6.
   1. Short stories, Australian. I. Dale, John, (A. John).
A823.0108

Cover photograph by Anne Zahalka, courtesy Roslyn Oxley9 Gallery
Cover design by Darian Causby

Printed in Australia by Griffin Paperbacks, Adelaide

7 6 5 4 3 2 1
99 98 97 96

Contents

Acknowledgements   vii
Introduction   ix

Dance of the Hunchbacks
Fiona McGregor   1

Manhunt
Garry Disher   31

The Devil in Ms Jones
Leonie Stevens   55

Pirates and Kings
Archie Weller   69

Four Poems
Les Murray   107

Just Us
Zyta Plavic   117

Barring Down
James McQueen   141

The Whippet and the Willow
Gillian Mears   161

Burial
Allan Donald   189

The Night of the Fruit-Pickers
Margaret Simons   205

End of the Road
Ann Dombroski   229

Contributors   257

Acknowledgements

The Editor wishes to thank Lyn Tranter, Louise Thurtell, Ann Dombroski and the University of Technology, Sydney.

Les Murray's poem 'It Allows a Portrait in Line Scan at Fifteen' first appeared in the *Times Literary Supplement*. Lyrics from 'Goin' Out West' by Tom Waits reproduced by permission of Warner/Chappell Music Australia Pty Ltd. Unauthorised copying is illegal.

Introduction

Like many Australians I grew up in the outer suburbs, on the edge of an expanding city. As the new roads, parades and crescents crept back over the hills, new families moved in. Footpaths were concreted, creeks filled in and lawns sown. We lived right at the end of the bus line and although we didn't have a car, we had the garage waiting for one. The city was a place you went to once a fortnight, while the bush lay a cracker's throw beyond the back fence. Dry sclerophyll country, but to everyone it was just bush. The outer suburbs were where things happened – murders, suicides, multiple car accidents – and though sometimes these 'tragedies', as they were called, made the six o'clock news, they were quickly forgotten. The smaller and often more intriguing stories that you heard about other families were passed on orally and never written down.

Now, some thirty years later, the suburbs have rolled back another twenty kilometres, the bush has retreated behind the hills, and the people out there on the edges still tend to be overlooked. It has been said that the bush is the traditional reservoir of distinctive Australian qualities, but for me and my friends it was the outer suburbs. That's where we grew up and that's where we tried to escape from.

In 1983 the editor of *Granta* magazine coined the term 'Dirty Realism' as a means of selling a group of new American writers to a British audience. Despite differences in style, these impressive new writers had two things in common. Firstly, they were writing about waitresses, construction workers, small-time thieves and door-to-door salespeople; ordinary blue-collar and lower middle class Americans unable to articulate their relationships and struggling with the exigencies of everyday life. Characters who drank and got divorced and kept on going. It was, as Bill Buford observed, a curious, dirty realism about the belly-side of contemporary life. The other important concern that linked writers such as Raymond Carver, Richard Ford, Bobbie Ann Mason, Tobias Wolff and Jayne Anne Phillips was the shift in focus from the major metropolitan centres of New York, Los Angeles and Chicago to the small towns and rural cities of middle America, places that make up the bulk of the American population.

In Australia, eighty-five per cent of the population live in urban areas; more than sixty-five per cent along the narrow east coastal sprawl that stretches from Geelong to Cairns. In our largest city two-thirds of the people live in the outer suburbs, yet so many of our stories are still set in small inner-city enclaves. 'Out West' is not a precise geographical location. It is not limited solely to the western suburbs of Sydney. The ten new stories and four poems in this collection cover a lot of turf and give voice to a part of Australia that is not often heard. People living in the small towns, the caravan parks, the satellite suburbs – people living on the edge.

Out West's intention is not to prescribe style or content for the short story, but rather to open up the fictional geography, to focus attention on places and people that don't get written about. If anything it is about a fictional redistribution. In an age when cable, CD-ROM and the Net compete for the reader's attention, it is even more important that the centuries old compact between writer and reader is adhered to: read this; you won't be disappointed. These stories won't disappoint. They are not bland. The men and women in this collection live in communes, mining towns, detention centres and suburban parks. They live in contemporary Australia.

As you would expect from eleven writers of diverse ages and background, and from right around the country, the styles vary. It would be presumptuous of any editor to categorise eleven distinct voices, though it may be true to say that the realism here is more dirty than dun-coloured, and the content is such that some critics might like to dismiss it as 'battler fiction'. But 'dirty realism' or 'battler fiction' – in the end these are only tags. The best fiction is about people, not abstractions, and in Australia a majority of the population live out there in the suburbs, on the edge of things. Sandwiched between the old bush yarns and the sophisticated inner-city tales of adultery and revolving dinner parties, stories from the outer suburbs have largely been ignored.

Raymond Carver said that good fiction is partly a bringing of the news from one world to another, that writing stories about particular kinds of people allows certain areas of life to be understood a little better than they were before. These four poems and ten stories do just that. They bring you the news from Nightcliff to Wollongong, from Perth to Somerville, from Grafton to Mulawa. They give voice to the men and women living on the edge of our great suburban sprawl.

OUT WEST – Australian Dirt.

John Dale

I'm gonna drive all night

Take some speed

I'm going out west

where they'll appreciate me

Tom Waits

Dance of the Hunchbacks

Fiona **McGregor**

The summer I turned thirteen I got braces, began to shave my legs, and my cousin Eddy came to stay. My one friend from school was away, so when Eddy had gone again the new pleasures of teenage were solitary and secretive. Now I had freedom I saw only its confines, and summer lagged on, an interminable ache of boredom, loneliness and hard little pieces of rubber the orthodontist pushed between my teeth in preparation for braces. Nights my family was out I played the cassettes from Eddy's collection as loudly as I could stand it, experimenting with kohl and eyebrow tweezers while I sang 'Stranded' to the bathroom mirror. Days I rode my bike to the shopping centre and back, freewheeling along the smooth hot paths in the dream of adventure brought by Eddy's music and the reality that it didn't exist here. I was thin and tanned, unhappy without really knowing it.

We lived on a hill looking south to where the Brindabellas rose yellow–brown in summer, turning bluer as winter advanced. Sometimes I'd wake to a white serrated horizon, or fog over the valley of red roofs, and imagine snow sweeping across the sheep-ruined land to the outer suburbs. The frost could get so thick we'd pretend it was snow, stamping swear words in it as we waited by the orange plastic bus-stop shelter at the bottom of the hill. Our house was brown, outside and in, pine or cane furniture and puce carpet everywhere, the velour lounge set patterned with brown stripes of varying shades and width. Brown and beige circles interlocked across the bathroom tiles; the toilet seat was fawn with a fawn fur cover. When I left four years later the interior of the house hadn't changed. But outside the wattles and gums on the nature strip were twice as high, and our neat native garden had grown, narrowing the view. Suburbs I'd never been to stretched below and my graffiti on the bus-stop shelter had long been updated.

Madeleine arrived halfway through second term, in the middle of the week. She wasn't in my class. She trailed behind Ivana to our corner of the quadrangle, cautious, insouciant, the sleeves of her maroon jumper pulled down over her hands. Her hair was thick and parted on the side so most of it hung over her face. She smelt of something sweet, warm and familiar.

Madeleine's father had bought a pub near Civic. Five storeys, she told us, sixty-four rooms; ladies lounge, saloon, public bar, dining-room, a beer garden and even an entrance foyer with a black grand piano. She lived there during the week, going to their country house on weekends, and I placed her immediately in a dark bar of my imagination, where she struggled through her homework in an atmosphere of sordid decay. She said she'd been to a convent all her life, the exclusive one on Sydney harbour, and that this Catholic high school was the best her parents could do for the time being in Canberra. Ivana trod hard on my toe and I sniggered into my lunch. We would have to corrupt Madeleine then: so much the better. Ivana reckoned she wouldn't survive long in that uniform, but I secretly admired the wrong black of Madeleine's stockings, the length of her maroon tunic, frigid and daggy on anyone else, mature on Madeleine. Maybe I was the only one who thought this – my tastes ran to black, and wrong – it was years before I realised the Preston twins meant it when they called Madeleine a fat dag.

Madeleine was one of the tallest girls in our form; she was as tall as my sister Jo, who was three years older. She didn't know what rags meant, although she had them once a month, unlike me. She never said 'grouse' or 'choice' and thought all the girls looked like sluts in their hiked-up uniforms, waiting at the bus-stop for their boyfriends to pick them up after school. Thirteen and doing it already, how off. Our time would come, I knew that. Ivana was beginning to preen herself, last year's tunic way undersize. But Miss, my parents can't afford a new one. She knew how to bung it on. I ate constantly but stayed thin, filling up with anger when I wanted to fill with lust like all the other girls. At night I explored myself under the bedcovers, wishing to unstop the blood and let childhood trickle away. I wanted the pain that Jo displayed, flaked out on the couch in front of 'Get Smart', groaning for a hot-water bottle. A cloud of plastic bags on the counter told me she'd restocked her corner of the fridge with skim milk, yoghurt, wheat-germ and yeast. I made her a hot-water bottle, thinking she really did look sick. She was even thinner than last week, and the romantic dark circles beneath her eyes had begun to bulge. I wondered why she wasn't hiding in her room, and asked her where The Invisible Man was.

'Haven't seen him. Ha!'

'What about Mum?'

'Out hunting for mascarpone to fatten up the virgins. She's probably picking up Dad from the orifice.'

'You mean picking him out of.'

'Yair right, Tina.'

The credits rolled and I took my cassette over to the stereo.

'"Bewitched"'s on next.' Jo looked at me stonily, a third glare coming from the pimple she'd been torturing in the middle of her forehead. I didn't have to do much to annoy her. Just breathe.

'Cyclops,' I said.

'Fucken brat!' The cushion bounced off my elbow as I left the room. I saw another fight looming where she would insist on her health drink for dinner, and my mother would finish in tears.

I cried in the midnight of my family sleeping, my walkman in bed with me blasting it all away. I had once tried to kill my sister; I was seven years old. I went into the bathroom with the breadknife to cut off her head, and she lay back in the bath, baring her throat. The knife didn't even graze her. She grabbed my arm and gave me a Chinese burn. Well, you asked for it! Still I dreamt of her death, the perfect antidote to her authority and our dull family life. Murder would be sweet catharsis but the scenes I imagined left me sick with fear. I knew if anyone could see inside my head I'd be locked up. Sometimes I rolled onto my walkman in my sleep: a jab between the shoulder blades and I was upright, awake, cold filtering through the window. Too old to believe it was wings sprouting to fly me out of there, too young to fly out in actuality, I lay in bed hating what I had been born into. I spent all my pocket money on batteries and my ears itched constantly from the imprint of headphone discs. I fell asleep late, singing, I thought, silently. But there were weird looks from the family in the morning. Comatose, I winced at their loud voices. Jo leaning in my doorway, 'I can *hear* you, y'know. And for your information, you sound pretty bloody stupid.' My mother in her tracksuit appearing behind with my hot chocolate. '*Basta*, Giovanna! *Sbrigati*, Christina. *Su!*'

5

I untangled myself from my headphones then went into the kitchen and snuck coffee into the hot chocolate. I put my fish skeleton earrings in my pencil case and changed out of my woggy gold sleepers on the bus.

Madeleine had a mouth perfect as a lipstick print. The sweet warm smell came from a miniature tub of lanoline she carried with her everywhere so her lips always shone. 'But jeez she gets on my nerves sometimes,' said Ivana. 'The way she just kinda looks at you and doesn't say anything. Little Miss Priss.'

I knew what she meant, Madeleine's restraint of approval, her mouth always closed yet moving slightly as though the words didn't taste good enough to be spoken. I said she was just shy; Ivana said we weren't good enough for her.

Absorbed in frenchplaiting Ivana's hair, I didn't see how the fight started. I heard Madeleine's enraged screams and looked up to see her trying to roll away from Janine Preston's kicking feet. I got up. 'You haven't tucked my flicks in, Tina,' Ivana reproached. 'Let them fight it out.' But I was walking purposefully towards the evil eye of Leanne Preston, guardian of her sister's scrag fights. I'd been bashed up by them before, I knew what they were capable of. Chunky, freckly, red-haired girls, the Prestons scared me and I had no idea what I was doing. Then they scattered, and Mr Leong was there, helping Madeleine get to her feet. Later Madeleine pretended it hadn't shaken her. Ivana and I pretended not to be impressed by her spirit.

Within a week the swelling had gone down and Madeleine was entertaining us. She could eat her fist – I thought of a boa constrictor dislocating its jaw to swallow prey whole – she could whistle between her teeth and a hard spear of water jetted between the two top ones onto the back of your neck when you were walking into class. She could roll her tongue into a tube and lick her nose. Contempt was a lifting of the top right-hand corner, disgust two fingers jabbed into its cavern, surprise the cavern alone. But it wasn't till a week afterwards, running across the oval, escaping the rain, that her mouth spoke my language. She sang in a low monotone and I recognised the words, then caught up and joined in the chorus of 'Psychokiller'. 'Better run run run run run run run a-waaayyy . . . !' And we ran like that, screaming at the sky.

'D'you want to?' I said another day as we shared a smoke in the toilets. 'Seriously?'

'Yep,' she nodded. 'I hate this school, I'm sick of my fucken parents. I hate this city.'

I put the cigarette out and we snuck out behind the netball courts, crunching tic-tacs. I could see the Preston twins coming, and pulled Madeleine down to hide. I said we could go on our bikes. Not all the way if it was too tiring – they let you put bikes on trains. We could ride to the station and put them on the train to Sydney. We had bikes, we had wheels, we could go anywhere. Money? Who cared? I could empty my piggy bank and Madeleine even had a bank account; she had shares her father had bought her when she was born. I could sell my christening bracelet, my Communion chain and my sleepers – they were twenty-four carat – I could get a fortune. Sydney was warm, we could sleep in a park or on a beach if we had to. And I could ring Eddy – he'd help us, he'd know what to do. I had run away before but never lasted beyond nightfall; this time I was serious.

Later that afternoon the Prestons got busted for smoking in the toilets.

We lost Ivana over the winter months, in that careless, cruel pubescent way. She always wanted to go to the dance which took place in the school hall at lunch-time once a fortnight. They played *Grease* and Abba and *Saturday Night Fever,* Madeleine and me sometimes coming as far as the doorway, doing the disgust jab while Ivana ventured inside. Up by the stage, teachers stood watching the kids dance awkwardly, taking it in turns to patrol the wings and dressing-rooms for teen sex. Ivana re-emerged one day with Fabio, a Year Ten boy, who said things to me in Italian that the girls didn't understand but guessed at by the way my face darkened. The school had recently gone from girls only to co-ed, and each term more boys appeared. They were still outnumbered and didn't have much trouble getting girlfriends. Talk about desperate.

That's what Madeleine said Ivana was. I didn't think she was, but I didn't defend her. I didn't look up when Ivana approached us at the bus-stop, not even when she was standing right in front of us. We acted like she wasn't there, but when she said she'd broken up with Fabio, Madeleine giggled.

'Wanna go to the movies tomorrow, Tina?' Ivana asked me.

I cringed from her desperate look and shifted my bag to the other shoulder, saying, 'I can't, I'm coming down with the flu,' at the same time as Madeleine said, 'She can't, she's coming to my house.'

Ivana backed away from our laughter and I turned and headed for the other end of the bus-stop, Madeleine trotting behind, still snorting with laughter. I didn't know why I felt like this; I didn't think leading would feel as bad as being led.

They were smooth and still, those Friday evening car trips through the pine forest and benighted sheep farms to Gundaroo. The car smelt of new upholstery and Mr Martin's cigars. He wore cream leather shoes with panels of fine plaiting and Mrs Martin always drove, one hand on the wheel, the other palm upwards on either shoulder, pushing her bob back into shape. Madeleine and me sat facing one another in the back, working through our repertoire of spastic faces.

Mrs Martin cooked fish fingers or chops with boiled potato and pumpkin. Sometimes there were a few leaves of lettuce, a slice of tomato and a slice of orange, with a bottle of Thousand Island dressing. The banality of this food was exotic to me. I loved its neat modern appearance. Our raspberry cordial turned purple in the tall pebbled blue glasses. We ate dinner in front of the television, Mr and Mrs Martin talking to one another without moving their eyes from the screen. They were so different to my parents: you didn't feel like you could fool them. No dinner table, no grace, and they both smoked, Mr Martin sometimes leaving his cigarette burning throughout the meal. 'And what does your father do, Tina?' he asked suddenly one night, making me jump.

'He works at the Department of Immigration.'

'Good Lord,' Mr Martin chuckled. 'He must work hard.'

'My mother used to work there too,' I added, thinking he was impressed.

'Oh really?' Mrs Martin examined me over the top of her glasses.

It hit me just before I had finished eating and I went into the bathroom to swear under my breath. Nailprints still marked my palms when Madeleine and I lay in bed talking after midnight, radio turned down low on the spindly table between our beds. Out here you could get no station without static, so we tuned into the shortwave frequencies and made faces to match the sounds, twisting bunches of our thick hair to look electric shocked.

One Saturday night I found a distant, fuzzy Double Jay, and we leaned towards the radio hungrily when they announced an hour with Radio Birdman. 'There's gonna be a new race,' Madeleine screeched while I strummed a guitar. 'The kids are gonna start it up!' Then she lay down and I continued: 'Ah'm gonna mu-tate!'

'Will you go to sleep!' Her mother was at the door.

'Don't worry about my parents,' whispered Madeleine when her mother had gone. 'They hate me even more.'

Another Saturday they had to go back to the hotel for a function and we had the house to ourselves. We got the Ramones from Madeleine's brother's bedroom and rampaged through the house in search of cigarettes. We found two Silk Cuts in her parents' room and smoked them as we went through every drawer in the house. Old dry-cleaning bills, batteries new and used, buttons, dust-caked sunglasses, hotel soaps, cufflinks. Until Madeleine called out and I ran into Julian's room to see what she'd found. A packet of B&H Special Filter. 'But it's only half full,' I said, disappointed.

'Oh durr.' Madeleine inserted two fingers between the cigarettes, then withdrew a foil packet. 'Marry-jewana,' she said, and continued the search until an orange juice bottle bong was discovered at the back of a cupboard. We did the Ministry of Silly Walks into the sunken living-room, me carrying the rest of Julian's record collection.

'D'you drink?' asked Madeleine, pouring herself a glass of cask wine.

'Yair. I got drunk with my cousin in the summer holidays.'

'I started drinking when I was twelve.'

'I started smoking when I was eleven. Or maybe ten. I reckon I'm getting addicted.'

'I didn't know you could get addicted to grass.'

'I was talking about smokes.'

'Oh. Julian started giving me cigarettes when I was eight.'

I told her about the day Eddy and I went into town to the movies, as we said to my parents. Eddy bought a cask and some glue then hot-wired a car in a lane behind Civic, and we went driving through the city, Eddy singing 'Smash It Up', passing me a joint. Within minutes we were lost in the leafy eastern suburbs, each street exactly like the one before, so many roads leading to nowhere. City of circuits and cul-de-sacs, we were dogs chasing our tails; the foliage through the windscreen spinning, my eyeballs rolling up. Eddy's dark woolly head was fading, and his skull ring on the steering wheel. At dusk he was shaking me. A cop car had passed and was doing a U-turn in the distance. Eddy got me out of the car, across the perfect lawns of two empty gardens, and over a fence. I hung onto him until my head cleared, and we found our way to a bus route.

Madeleine had stopped plaiting her hair and was watching me intently. 'Did you two do it?'

'Do what?'

'You know.'

'God Madeleine, he's my *cousin*!'

'So what. I kissed one of my cousins once. It was quite nice actually.' Four perfect smoke rings disappeared inside one another above her head.

'Have you ever done it?' I asked her.

'Done what?'

'You know.'

'Oh. You mean *fucked*. No. But I want to.'

I put on the Sex Pistols and pogoed around the bean bags. Madeleine writhed on the beige pile. With her electric hair and her lips cracked and darkened with shiraz she looked savage, and I leapt on top of her. She threw me off, screaming, and we wrestled like that until suddenly she became serious, bent forward. She was throwing up in the toilet when I discovered, at the back of the stack of records, one I'd never seen before: 'IGGY RAW POWER' in dripping horror movie letters. Mouth and eyes outlined in kohl, he stalked the stage in tight silver hipsters, howling demonically, red pupils glowing. Outside, a burst of currawong song as the sun sank lower behind the broccoli heads of trees on distant hills. Then the house was silent. I placed the record on the turntable. It was like being kick-started, a thrill jagging my spine at this voice like a skidding car in a jungle of guitars and heavy rhythm. I felt desperate and sated, as though my body had found its craving. Then Madeleine was there, hitting me with a pillow. There were other Stooges records going back to 1970, and we played them one after the other then began again from the beginning, deep pulse rippling through the still country night. We opened the drapes and danced to the double image of ourselves in the glass doors with the night glimmering behind. Opened a can of beer and with the ring pull cut our thumbs, pressed them together and swore lifelong allegiance. Blood still ran as we danced to a frenzy, spun out to the patio, attacking the lemon trees under the brilliant strip of stars. We were gods with our golf-stick guitars, gyrating around the pool blotched by the dead leaves of winter.

Headlights appeared on the road below, tipped over the crest of the hill so their outer sphere touched the house, and we hunched over to hide, dancing back inside, dancing with our shadows.

My hangover was a slowness, an acute sensitivity numbed by a secret afternoon bong. I knew I was ill but it felt like euphoria. Madeleine's parents arrived and took us back to Canberra in that prussian-blue Mercedes where a cassette of the Brandenburg concertos turned interminably. And now that I believed in the capacity of music to transform my landscape I saw the pine trees become the horns, the woodwind and brass; the strings were mist wreathed around them, trailing into the dark valleys, and I sat there silent for the hour-long drive, touching my swollen thumb, reawakening the pain.

Later in the week when the Martins went back to the house they found a piece of pizza in their bed, melted ice-cream under it and a red wine stain on the living-room carpet. The lemon trees looked stripped. They didn't believe our stories of marauding possums. Julian noticed the absence of his cigarette packet and punched Madeleine for that. She said it hurt to talk. I wanted to see her, bruised martyr, she seemed so bad the way she kept getting hit. But she was grounded for two weeks then got the flu, and by the time I saw her again she looked just like she had before: pretty, plump and utterly self-possessed.

The Invisible Man wondered if she were the reason for my recent bad marks. 'Fifteen per cent less than last term,' he said, antennae quivering from his crown. My mother fussed over these last hairs, desperately scraping them from the sides up across his baldness, and my father submitted absent-mindedly as he read the paper or poured more coffee. I said the work was harder than last term and maybe I just wasn't gifted academically. I tried to see his eyes but they gazed as ever at some invisible spot on the wall, some distant place inside him. My father perched on the edge of my mustard yellow bed as though the room was caving in on him. I knew he had only come into my room because my mother had told him to. The way he obeyed her filled me with contempt. I put my hand to my face over the ache in my molars, squeezed and stretched in new directions since that morning. My father told me quietly that my schoolwork was nothing now compared to what it would be in the final two years, and I would complete those final two years, because even if I got married I needed an education. Maybe I would become a secretary. Maybe even a teacher. Maybe, if I wanted and tried enough, I'd go to university. But I didn't want to be like Jo, who spoke more and more like a textbook. My father talked over a crunching outside my window: my mother pretending to weed her *orto* as she checked that he was disciplining me. I watched her delicate figure bending to the leeks and wondered why parents insisted you do exactly what they did and what they didn't manage to do as well. My parents hadn't finished school, so I didn't see why I had to.

Madeleine was an hour late. My worry fermenting to resentment, I stalked my narrow room, attached to my walkman: another aural blood transfusion of Iggy and the Stooges. The doorbell rang, then Jo's bedroom door slammed, then silence, then subdued voices. Madeleine was talking to my mother in her best voice, the one she used with her parents, the one she had brought to Canberra but learnt to banish from the playground. Suddenly I felt scruffy. I picked the earth from beneath my fingernails, brushed my hair, messed it up again. Madeleine burst into my room. 'You didn't tell me your mother was from Milan!'

'My father was born here though,' I said quickly.

'Well don't get all defensive. Milan's a fashion capital.'

The outer suburbs of Milan, housing commission, and she'd emigrated when she was thirteen: fashion didn't have much to do with my mother's upbringing, not judging by the 1972 velvet bellbottoms she still wore six years later. Domestic attire was always a tracksuit, the gardening one dark purple. She loved Madeleine's new red tap shoes and asked question after question, hands in her giant gardening gloves held away from her body, then directed Madeleine to the jar of amaretti before going back outside to greet Mrs Kotsinos. Any minute now there'd be an inspection of the new washing-machine cover, chosen to match the toilet cover. I had to get Madeleine out of here.

This was all we ever did – rode to the shopping centre – where else was there to go? Tuggeranong Lake was too far and besides, nature was boring. As spring wore on the magpies multiplied, swooping down on our two figures moving across the dry exposed playing fields. We ducked and swiped at them, invisible against the vast blue sky. Even the weather seemed motionless, sunny for weeks, still cold, although the sunsets I saw from my bedroom window looked so hot they might have been fake. It was like Toyland around here, everything new, no cracks in the paths, nothing out of place. We wanted to play with it, to zoom our bikes up and down, but like Toyland its appeal to two de-mented girls with a taste for harsh music was limited. We laughed at it, we laughed at everything. We laughed ourselves sick, each encounter hysterical. We dissolved disprins in Coke before drinking it, then waited to see what happened. We squashed into photo booths and pulled the weirdest faces possible. Alongside surreal sayings in our own private language, obscenities and band names, we pasted these photos into our diaries, ownership of them alternating. Our ambition was to visit every photo booth in Canberra.

It was Madeleine's set of photos today, and she snatched the narrow strip when it slid out of the machine, then looked at me in exasperation. 'You shouldn't open your mouth.'

My Choo-Choo-bar-pasted braces flashed darkly, my hair was like a golliwog's. 'I thought the idea was to look weird and ugly. What's it matter?'

'You're supposed to look weird and *funny*, Tina. Not necessarily *ugly*.'

I sucked my metal overbite and turned away. My surroundings made me feel even uglier. Woolies, Fosseys, pebbled cement and plastic benches, baby ghost gums in woodchip garden beds just like our front yard, a tiered fountain clogged with Chiko Roll packets. 'What are we gonna do now?' I said sulkily.

'How should I know?' Madeleine shrugged. 'You're the one who invited me over.'

'Rightio. Let's go into town.'

The bus terminated at Woden Plaza and the next one for Civic didn't leave for half an hour. We hung around the terminal, watching the people. 'They all look so *bored*.'

'They look like I feel.'

'Who's bored, them or us? Maybe it's just us, and we've got boredom lenses.'

'Nah, it's them, and they've infected us.'

'They look like they got into the washing-machine with their clothes on.' I started to swing around the bus-stop signposts. Madeleine joined in and we swung faster and faster, chasing and being chased, then came face to face with a conductor who told us to move along if we couldn't keep still. So we went up to the plaza through the gauntlet of sharpie gangs in desert boots and flannelette shirts, jeering at our clothes, calling us molls and asking us if we wanted a root.

'No thanks,' sang Madeleine, 'I grow my own.' And we took off past the escalators, them yelling they wouldn't want to fuck us anyway seeing as we were such molls. We spent the last of our money on soft serves and fried donuts, losing our bearings in the fluorescent labyrinth of shops of cheap T-shirts and vinyl shoes. 'Look Narelle, these'd roolly suit you.' Madeleine pointed to some white stilettos. Then I decided it was time to frighten some children, so we sat beside a plastic palm with our eyelids and lips turned inside-out, rotating our heads slowly. Then we did the Ministry of Silly Walks along to the escalator and up to Sussan's where I, lopsided, asked if they had pants for people with one leg longer than the other and Madeleine, bent double, asked if they had jackets for hunchbacks. 'God you're prejudice,' she said when the manageress told us to leave. Outside the accessories shop Madeleine opened her palm to reveal a pair of tiger eye studs, telling me I was going to pierce her ears later.

We went into David Jones and made ourselves up at the Revlon counter, blue eyeshadow on the right eyelid, green on the left, a bright red circle on each cheek. Madeleine drew a swastika on my forehead and I drew a peace sign on hers. 'Can I help you?' A shop assistant hovered and as we walked away, remarked to the cashier, 'Little tarts.' So we nicked some razor blades from pharmaceuticals and went up to the second floor to inspect every rack of clothes with bladed hands, chins pressed to chests to block the giggles and the fear. The store was closing when we reached ground floor again, carnage in our wake. There was a scattering sound and Madeleine was running out the doors, beads flying everywhere. I ran out the doors opposite, heart beating, palms sweating, wondering if we'd find each other down in the darkened car park, wondering how we'd get home without bikes or money.

'How can you listen to that crap! It's so aggressive, so . . . *sexist*,' said Jo, who liked reggae and Joni Mitchell, and always had a few fettuccine-thin plaits in her long hair, beaded at the bottom. She didn't approve of Madeleine either, since the time I'd served minestrone steaming through parmesan and Madeleine had reared back, 'Eugh, it smells like vomit!' Jo said Madeleine used me. She described the scene to my parents when they came home from the Kotsinos. They were suspicious of Madeleine after that, always polite and welcoming, yet suspicious, and nervous – maybe even a bit afraid. They never let me stay at her parents' pub. I had to lie I was going to Gundaroo.

I was in love with Iggy Pop; his lyrics and smooth body, his dark voice and music. Inside it I was fearless, my world condensed to a sleazy metropolis where I roamed the streets, tough and strong. Julian put 'Lust for Life' on the public bar jukebox, and if his parents weren't there and Madeleine and I picked up glasses, he let us watch the bands that he booked on weekends. We went to bed late, me lying awake with excitement. Sometimes, looking across at her sleeping face, I panicked I would lose Madeleine. I imagined natural catastrophes, car accidents and crimes, and I thought if I had to choose one person in the world to survive with me, it would be her.

She disappeared one night when I was cleaning my teeth, then reappeared with two schooners of ice. 'You have to sterilise the safety pin first,' she said, holding ice to her ear with a pale blue washer. I held the pin over a match and then pushed it through. Her lobes were large and fleshy, the unfrozen centre resisting, my fingertips sliding around blood and moisture. 'God you fucken hurt me!' She cupped a hand over her ear and glared at me. She didn't hide her sadistic pleasure as I had mine when she pierced my left lobe with the other tiger eye stud. She placed it adjacent to my first hole, and I watched her eyes changing as the metal entered my flesh, the inner circles of rust that pulsed in her grey iris when she twisted the bedside lamp, how she receded behind these eyes while her face came closer. Then the side of my head was on fire and we were toasting our new piercings with stolen beer and cigarettes.

We slept in a room at the end of the corridor on the fourth floor. Madeleine knew where the keys to the chips and chocolate machines were. I watched from the window the comings and goings in the hotel car park while she was downstairs replenishing our supplies. A constant stream of people and everything was old; the buildings, the footpaths, even the trees. In here, life was rich. But we knew it could be even richer and sat cross-legged on the pale green chenille bedspreads making up new words and faces, whinge-ing about school and family, planning our trip away.

I lost Madeleine one Friday night, picking up glasses when the band had finished playing. Sticky arc balanced against my torso, I roamed through the crowded bar and the ladies lounge, mouth shut to hide my braces, and found her finally out in the beer garden, talking to a stranger. She didn't introduce me to him but I sat there anyway, staring at her shoulders, not knowing where else to go. He left quite suddenly, before the pub had closed. When I asked Madeleine why, she rolled her eyes and said he was probably gay.

Showtime in the sunken living-room at Gundaroo, I let the needle drop gently on the record then ran to the light switch, turning the dimmer slowly as the synthetic percussion of 'Heart of Glass' tinkled across the fire-place stage. Madeleine drifted out from the dark kitchen in a pearl slip of her mother's and high strappy Charles Jourdan shoes. She was Debbie Harry, hanging onto the mantelpiece, crooning into a pepper grinder, an angry ear lobe poking through her hair. I felt shy. It was like seeing her naked. Outlines of her nipples and navel visible through the fabric, smooth convexity of her belly. I cheered from the beanbag in the corner, sweating crescent moons in anticipation of my show. I drew kohl around my eyes and mouth and stripped down to tight ripped jeans, then strode bare-chested into the living-room to the metallic chaos of The Stooges. 'I am the world's forgotten boy, the one who search-es and destroooys!' Madeleine smoked on the couch. I felt her eyes cold on my button mushroom nipples, and turned to sing to the windows, then turned back again and jumped on the couch, straddling her. 'Gimme danger, little stranger. Gimme danger, little stranger.' One of my rubber bands popped out and hit her on the forehead.

'God you're rough!' Madeleine extricated herself and turned the music down. 'You're only supposed to do one song, Tina. And I'm sick of that band, they're so old. They've broken up.'

'But Iggy's just put out "Lust for Life"!'

'Woopy-do.'

'Well you don't have to get shitty.' I sat hunched forward in the beanbag, wanting to cover myself, and Madeleine went into the kitchen to get another Tim Tam. 'Ya don't hafta get shitty,' I heard her say faintly, mimicking my accent. I hugged my knees tighter, wanting to go outside. To walk back to Canberra along the dark winding road with her white figure following me, calling me back. Then she was leaning in the doorway, man's jumper over the pearl slip, biscuit in hand, saying as though I was crazy, 'Tina, come and watch telly. Don't *sulk*.'

Her sisters were there the next day in their high heels and fine gold jewellery, unpacking dips and salads, putting chips into bowls. They made us watch television in the study while the party was on. Madeleine was furious, arguing all day, crying in her bedroom. I wanted to go back to Canberra, but Madeleine was determined. She stole a packet of No-Doz from one sister, and a cask of moselle from the fridge. We couldn't feel the pills, so we took three more. Later, I went to the toilet and when I got back the study was empty. The corridor lengthened and twisted as I walked down it and into the kitchen, so bright, so loud, all those strangers staring at me. I concentrated on finding the next hard surface to hang onto. I passed people dancing to the Saints in the dining-room, Julian calling me, holding out a bong. I sat down and smoked it, hearing someone ask how old I was, giggling.

Then I saw Madeleine outside by the pool, swaying in the arms of a man. He was tall, he seemed ancient as I approached. Then I was hugging him, the pool looming on the edge of my vision, their four eyes looking down at me. 'Madeleine, I couldn't find you . . .' This voice wasn't mine. The man steered me inside and I collapsed on the couch in the emptying living-room, arms covering my face. I saw him twist the armchair to face the fake fire then sit in it and pull her on top of him. I watched the back of the chair. Raised my head slightly to hear them, a cramp in my neck beginning almost immediately. I kept my arms over my face. I feigned sleep. Madeleine's head rose and she looked straight at me, an unfocused, distant, smiling gaze, then she lowered her head alongside his, her shoulders heaving back and forth, and I watched through streaming eyes, fighting the pain that took hold of my neck, my shoulders, my back, my entire body.

I saw them talking up the other end of the locker-room while we changed for P.E. Their low urgent exchange could have been an argument but felt more like a barrier as I walked up to say hello.

'Oh!' Madeleine turned with her hand on her chest. 'You gave me a fright.'

Ivana said nothing.

'Youse going to P.E.?' I asked.

'Oh, probably not,' Madeleine said lightly, and began to peel a mandarin. I noticed she had taken her earring out.

'Yair, it's so hot,' I said. 'I couldn't be fucked.'

Ivana jutted her face forward. 'No, you couldn't, could you?' And they snorted into their lockers, the other girls turning to see what had happened.

I was crying again, into the kitchen sink. My night to wash up and we'd had melanzane. I picked and scrubbed, tears streaming onto the crusty pyrex dish. My mother heard me and came in. '*Che cosa c'é?*' Taking me by the shoulders, turning me towards her. '*Ma* Christina, *che cosa c'é che non va?*' My father offered me chocolate. 'Alright?' He rubbed my back.

'What's wrong, Christina?' I cringed with embarrassment, convulsing with tears. Then Jo came in, brushing
her hair.

'*Non in cucina*!' my mother reprimanded, and
snatched Jo's brush from her.

'Can I go horse riding, Mum? It's only thirty dollars
a lesson, and I can get a lift with Melinda. What's
wrong with Tina?' she said, seeming irritated.

'Dancing *or* horse riding,' said my father. 'We can't
afford both.'

'God.' Jo turned, her hair spinning out around her.
'You spend a *fortune* on Tina's teeth, which is just a
cosmetic indulgence, and I'm not even allowed to do
something that's *good* for me.'

'I never said I wanted braces!' I yelled after her.

'Maybe I'll just hang around the plaza smoking and
sniffing glue like some of the other disaffected youth
around here!' she yelled back, then slammed her door.

My father went after her and my mother took me
in her arms. I howled and pushed her away, clutching
my ear. She threw her arms in the air at the sight of
my new earring, and I fled to my bedroom, my
mother in pursuit, crying now as well.

Later I knocked softly on Jo's door to borrow a
black texta. 'Did it hurt?' she asked.

'Nuh.' I lifted my hair.

'Eeughh, choice . . . it's got pus everywhere.'

'It just stings a bit. It'll go down.'

'God you're dumb. You know it means you're a
lesbian when you've got two earrings in one ear.'

'Oh sure. What about Eddy?'

'Oh, my hero.'

'Anyhow, you're the lesbian feminist. You listen to Joan Armatrading. Talk about daggy.'

'You need a psychiatrist.'

'You're the anorexic one.'

On my way out, I made an ugly tongue and braces face at her.

'God you're immature,' she sighed.

Five years later Madeleine would be raped by three men at the Cross. They would grab her near the fountain and do it on the edge of Fitzroy Gardens late one Friday night, passers-by probably thinking it was a rough trick. She would tell me about this not twenty-four hours after it happened when I ran into her at Central Station. Me in my combat boots and Kill City T-shirt, my sugar-watered hair, a relic at seventeen because it was 1983 and the music I loved, and its culture, had been polished and honed to something I barely recognised. I had been living in Sydney two years and hadn't seen Madeleine for four. She was plump as ever in autumn browns. But her eyes had changed to loose nervous discs, shot through with broken blood vessels. I towered over her now; she seemed so vulnerable. She told me about the night before immediately we said hello, in a high panting laugh, then ran to catch a train. And as I stood there looking around me at the passengers, the ticket collectors and news-stand, everything became still and dark like a black and white photo, a feeling I would experience again, and again, when people I knew began to die.

When she turned from me I saw a blood-red bruise along the back of her neck, counterpoint to her collar. It occurred to me she had liked me because I was different, then had no longer liked me for the same reason.

But this was before then, it was the summer I turned fourteen, when I still believed we'd be friends forever, when I still imagined us bike-riding the highway to Sydney in a 'Lust for Life' soundtrack. My teeth were lined up ready to be revealed and I had put up ads in the supermarket for work cleaning and babysitting. Madeleine was booked into the grammar school. She had stopped returning my calls, but I blamed it on her parents, then as the weeks went by I told myself she must have gone away. Until the day Jo came home and told me she'd seen Madeleine coming out of a cinema with two boys and a girl. I didn't think it would be so hard to run into someone in such a small city and I caught the bus to Civic whenever I could. Hung around the shops, avoided David Jones, walked up and down past the Martins' hotel.

That Saturday afternoon melted into my memory, and set, like hot metal. No wind, sun high in a hard blue sky, so hot I imagined my ripple soles flattening while I stood on the asphalt in the stark city centre, wondering what to do. The trees were scorched and wilted; shadows so sharp I flinched when I crossed their threshold. I sought refuge in the library and read magazines for a couple of hours. Then I decided to photocopy my face and send it to her.

I waited by the machine until the librarian disappeared behind some shelves, then lay my face on the glass and pulled the thick rubber mat around my head. I crossed my arms over the back of my neck to block out the light. Cocooned in chemical darkness, I felt my dry lips split and open as the coin dropped into the slot. A white-hot flash and a warm saltiness seeping through my teeth. I stood and licked the blood off my bottom lip as the image spat into the tray. I stared at this face that faintly resembled mine. It looked as though I was being held down. It looked as though I was drowning.

Manhunt

Garry **Disher**

Lyn is thinking about names – her own, her husband's, their baby daughter's, the gang in the Somerville pub – when Craig's hand slips from her shoulder to her breast, squeezing that engorged flesh in front of everybody. She flinches. 'Lyn' is short for Lynette. Craig is just Craig. Their friends at the Somerville pub include a Trina, an Ian, a Debra, a Brett and another Lyn. When it was clear that Craig wouldn't be bringing his mind to bear upon the subject of a name for the baby, Lyn told the midwives to write down Nina Elizabeth; Elizabeth after Craig's mother. A midwife skilled at calligraphy prepared a name-card and sticky-taped it to Nina's bassinet, a clear plastic tub which at this moment is reclining on a chrome trolley back at the hospital, Nina swaddled in pink, only her little head showing. Lyn wonders how often the midwives at the Bush check for arrested breathing. She wonders if her daughter needs changing, needs a feed, needs some loving attention. Craig's hand relaxes, tightens again.

Lyn has never known it to be so smoke-ridden and deafening in the Somerville pub – unless her senses are more acute after the birth, after the cloistered peace of the hospital. Susannah, in the room next to Lyn's at the Bush, was going to Suko Thai for her evening out. Suko Thai is just across from the hospital, not miles along some dirt road way the other side of Dare's Hill. Lyn knows *why* Craig chose the Somerville pub tonight – he wanted a distraction from his creeping fears – but why couldn't *she* have been that distraction, instead of his mates? Still, the dark cloud is lifting from him a little. He's shouting down the scoffers that he wanted a girl all along. Then his hand cups Lyn's breast again. She can picture the cheery glint in his eyes, a kind of challenge to everyone, but her nipples are so painful she could cry. The girls seem to know. Like peas in a pod across the table from Lyn, they're looking on avidly, curiously, a little enviously. This is the first baby in their crowd, which to Lyn is all the more reason why her baby daughter should have a head start in life, a name rare, cosmopolitan and exquisite, so that with any luck she'll never get stuck in one of the Somerville pubs of the world.

Lyn shifts, unmistakably shaking off her husband's hand. He gives her a kidding look. 'What's up with you all of a sudden?'

'I'm sore, Craig. You know that.'

It sometimes seems to Lyn that she spends half her life making Craig feel better. After a while she leans against him again. There is no padding on the bench seats in the booths at the Somerville pub. What with an episiotomy and fourteen hours of straining in the birthing suite four days ago, Lyn's anus, vulva and all the flesh around them are battered and bruised. She aches, she feels heavy down below. This morning she passed a blood clot the size of an egg, catching it in a specimen tray. The midwife on duty poked at it suspiciously but didn't say anything. Why didn't she say anything? According to Susannah, you can buy inflatable ring-cushions in the chemist's opposite the tractor dealership. Lyn took two Panadol before coming out tonight. She rests her hand on Craig's thigh, playing a waiting game. It works. Soon he's accommodating her, his bony chin rasping on the crown of her head.

'Sorry,' he says. 'Keep forgetting.'

Owing to a sensation in her nipples akin to being sliced open by razor blades, Lyn has been expressing milk for Nina. It's carefully labelled and stored in freezer bags, rows of tiny whitish slabs ready for thawing. The midwives laugh kindly when they hook Lyn to the breast pump, joke about the electric humming, tell her that dignity flies out the window when a woman has a baby. Craig has twice witnessed this indignity in Lyn's room, turning his head away, helpless, hunted, a little squeamish-looking.

So squeamish that he wouldn't attend the birth. 'Can't stand the sight of blood,' he said. Unlike Susannah's partner, Athol. Athol and Susannah are not married, that's Lyn's guess. Athol attended all of the antenatal classes and stayed right through the birth, holding Susannah's hand, massaging her neck, supporting her on the birthing stool, the loo, the adjustable bed. Athol and Susannah fascinate Lyn.

'You're going where?' Susannah had said, appalled, catching Craig and Lyn as they left the Bush earlier.

Certainly not the Suko Thai. Lyn imagines a table for two. She imagines walking there from the hospital, not bouncing over the back roads in a ute. Champagne, a candle in the centre of a white tablecloth – that's what the midwives of the Pandowie Bush Nursing Hospital have in mind when they urge you to have an evening out – *last chance!* – before you go home with the baby and your life changes forever.

Not the beer slop, pokies, scratch band, smoke and noise of the Somerville pub.

At least it's taking Craig's mind off things. He's laughing, shouting, talking again, a booming within his chest that strikes sympathetic vibrations inside her own ribcage. A big man full of life. Lyn tenses: a tingling, hardening rush in her breasts. Her milk is coming. She waits for the sensation to pass.

Across the table from her, Ian winks. 'So, all that kicking and it was a ballet dancer after all.'

Lyn says, quick as a flash, 'Or a footballer.' It's something Susannah would have said. Lyn feels oddly pleased with herself. Then she sees their expressions, half-comprehending, and thinks: Well, that went over like a lead balloon.

Craig roars, 'To my kid, ruck-rover for Pandowie!'

They wave their glasses in the air. 'Ruck-rover!'
'Kirstie!'

Their voices trail away. They watch Lyn and Craig, anticipation not far from the surface.

'Craig, her name is Nina.' Quietly, intently, she says, 'We've been through all this. Are you saying you want to change it now?'

He shrugs. 'Nina's fine.'

Lyn watches his face closely. She decides to hold her tongue. She doesn't want to get into an argument – not about this, not here, not tonight. 'Sweetheart, can we go now? I should be getting back.'

Debra says kindly, 'You must be tired.'

Craig grumbles his way out of the booth, Lyn easing her sore behind along the bench seat after him. She stands. The lights spin, and the lounge – as broad, fumy, racketing, cluttered and crowded as a woolshed – tilts and sways. Craig puts a hand under her elbow. 'Whoops! Thought I'd lost you there for a minute.'

'*See ya!*' the others cry. '*Love to the baby!*'

They collide with Brett, coming back from the Men's. 'Hey, Linnie,' he slurs, working eyebrows and mouth, 'you want to watch yourself, going home with this bloke. He was on "Crimestoppers" last week. You know, "armed and dangerous, approach with caution".'

Craig lunges, pinning Brett against the wall. 'You rotten bastard.'

All the jokiness fades from Brett's face. 'Mate, I'm sorry, didn't mean anything by it, just a joke, honest.'

Lyn tugs at her husband's arm. 'Craig? Leave it, come on, he's a fool, not worth worrying about.'

But the two men are jaw to jaw. Lyn can feel her heart hammering. 'Craig, please?'

Finally Craig swats the air dismissively with his hand and backs away. 'Fucking moron.'

'Mate, what can I say? I'm sorry, all right?'

Craig pushes forward again. 'Wasn't me, okay? I was nowhere near the place.'

Brett puts up both hands. 'Craig, mate, I know it wasn't you. I was just sounding off, okay? Mate?'

'Craig? Shake his hand, come on, he didn't mean it.'

Part of Lyn's life with Craig consists of dodging storms. She watches the two men make up, then leads him quickly out of the pub. They step into a vast summer night hung with stars. She looks up, drawing in great gulps of air scented with harvest dust, diesel and the irrigated soil of the lucerne flats. Somerville hugs the earth. There's nothing to break the starry dome but the wheat silos and the pines around the cemetery, like clean black shapes snipped out of tin. Otherwise the endless universe is empty.

These past few months, Lyn's emotions have come flooding out of nowhere, leaving her stunned. 'I want to drop by home,' she says suddenly. Her baby is waiting, her calm pastel-green room in the Bush, but Lyn wants to see her house again and stand for a moment in each of the rooms, especially the little one she's prepared for Nina at the end of the passage. She wants to touch the nursery-rhyme frieze on the wall and set the woodland-creatures mobile dipping and swaying from the ricepaper light in the ceiling.

'Ah, sweetheart, you're too tired.'

Lyn sets her jaw: 'I want to.'

Craig bends to unlock the ute. He climbs in behind the wheel and pushes the passenger door open for her. She slides in. Road dust, turpentine, vinyl, Craig himself, even a trace of Bluff, familiar odours from her life before the baby. Something sure has happened to her sense of smell. What she can't get enough of at the hospital is the scent of Nina's little skull. A touch of perfumed soap now, but until yesterday there had been fine clottings of vernix still caught in the wispy hair, rich and sweet and natural and like nothing she'd ever smelt before, like something you'd want to bottle.

'Just a little while,' she says. 'Can't we? Please?'

'What about, you know, the baby, Nina?' – 'baby' and 'Nina' a little foreign on his tongue.

'The midwives will look after her. That's what they're there for.'

Craig cranks the weary motor into life, yanks the column shift into first. Gravel crunches under the tyres and then they're out of the car park and shuddering along the Pandowie road. The altitude light on Dare's Hill winks palely red, a warning to bush pilots. Lyn has a sense of her smallness, the white Falcon a crawling speck in the black reaches of space.

'It's a bit of a shambles, home, okay?'

'I don't care.'

'Haven't had time to clean up, what with you, work, Bluff, etcetera.'

'Don't worry about Bluff. He'll come back.'

Craig shakes his head, greenish in the lights of the instrument panel. 'Nup. Some bastard's nicked him.'

The road is badly corrugated. The locals joke that there are only two comfortable speeds on such a road, a dead stop or flat out.

A couple of years ago Craig wouldn't have cared two hoots about the road, but he's become a scowling holder of opinions in the last few months. He'd like to give the bastards in Canberra a run for their money. As he says, a Labor government would never spend a cent on a district that voted Liberal, and a Liberal government wouldn't spend a cent because it wouldn't need to, no matter how ratshit the roads got.

'Please? Just for a little while? It'll make me feel better. I want to see Nina's room.'

'Aaah,' Craig says, hunching over the wheel. 'Don't say I didn't warn you.'

The house is one of the fierce attachments of Lyn's existence. The others are Craig and now Nina. It's taken her two years to get to this point. She doesn't want to go back to that old life, not enough money coming in, always on the move from one rented house to the next. Those houses always smelt damp, even in mid-summer. They sat on rotting stumps. They crouched among nettles on back roads miles off the beaten track or near the cemetery or the quarry or the dump. They had outside toilets – stifling, tilting fibro boxes that housed redbacks, the grime of the ages and the accumulated muck of all the tenants before you.

'Have the police been again?'

'Nup.'

Craig's manner seems to say: *But they will.* It's an attitude he's developed over the years, an expectation that if anyone's going to be blamed or suspected, he is. Lyn hasn't been able to convince him that the police were obliged to question everyone. 'Don't worry,' she says. 'You weren't even there.'

Not there when a stud manager's wife got raped and shot on a station property east of Dare's Hill. Lyn can't recall where Craig had said he'd been when it happened – painting the new portables at the high school? Something like that. But the thing was, he had been out there earlier in the week, painting the homestead roof. That's why the sergeant from Burra and a detective from Adelaide had come knocking, why they'd confiscated Craig's little .22, even though he hasn't fired it in all the time Lyn has known him.

'Anybody could've done it,' she says. 'Some of those places out there employ a dozen people.'

But he had been there, and he had come home dog-tired all that week, ranting and raving about how stuck-up they were, treating him like dirt. To distract him she'd tried pressing his hand to her stomach wall to remind him that he had a little treasure on the way – not that Nina had necessarily obliged with a kick or a stretch.

'Craigie, they'll do a test and prove it wasn't your gun.'

What she doesn't say is: *Unless they're thinking you used a gun no one knows about.*

'So what? They've got to pin it on someone. Why not me?'

'Craigie, don't.'

They stare ahead, along the probing headlights. Suddenly they're on smooth bitumen, the tyres settling into a low growl beneath them. Lyn realises she's been bracing herself for the past fifteen minutes, protecting her poor insides from the corrugated dirt, one hand tight on the dashboard. She relaxes a little. Big brash signs leap at them from the roadside: *Selling now! Pandowie Country Estate. House and Land Packages from $79,999.*

The road loops down into what used to be the Elders–G.M. stockyards. It's now a scraped-bare huddle of thirty-five tract homes dotted along freshly tarred streets. Lyn and Craig live in Waratah Court, a cul-de-sac in the corner by the racecourse. When Lyn was seven months pregnant she'd gone out every day for three weeks looking for a house to buy, tired of renting, the place they were in too cramped for a baby. It wasn't as if they had to go on renting. She had her two-and-a-half days a week as a teachers' aide at the primary school and Craig was picking up one painting contract after another, what with the district taking off. New houses, new businesses, the TAFE College where Susannah and Athol are lecturers, more kids at the high school, tourists coming through to see the rock paintings out east, the miners' dugouts in the Pandowie Creek. Lyn and Craig spoke to the manager at the Commonwealth, and two weeks before the murder, ten days before Nina was born, they moved into Waratah Court.

Lyn places her hand on Craig's thigh as he approaches their driveway. The Estate is a region of raw dirt and new brick, badly in need of lawns and gardens and kids' bikes, but Lyn loves it. Craig spins the wheel, the headlights dip for a moment, the ute bumps squarely onto the cement forecourt.

And she leans forward, appalled. 'What are those tins doing there?'

'I been flat out, you wouldn't believe.'

'Oh, Craig.'

He's turned the carport into a workshop. Ladders, tins of paint and brushes are scattered over paint-speckled tarps. 'You're supposed to use the shed. What if you have a spill? Jesus, Craig.'

He turns on her, flashing. 'Always something, isn't there? Always something you've got an opinion on.'

Lyn chokes, a succession of sobs coming out of nowhere, racking her swollen frame. She can't speak. Craig flings himself out of the ute and slams the door behind him, a concussion in her ears. He stalks to the edge of the darkness, bellowing, 'Bluff! Bluffy! Here boy!' After a while, Lyn climbs blindly onto the glassy cement. She gulps and blinks. That's all she can do – Craig's got the house keys.

He returns to the light, shouldering past her to the screen door. She hears its tinny squeak, sees a square of notepaper flutter onto the welcome mat by her sandalled feet.

Lyn's too sore, too tired, too posed in misery to bend for it. She tugs mutely on Craig's belt, points, watches him scoop up the note and read it.

A low, suffering, reflexive moan. He sways in pain. 'Craigie?'

'I told you. What did I tell you? They won't let go.'

She takes the note from his fist. He slides the key into the front door lock, letting the screen door bang against his narrow hip, sealing her from him, as she reads: '9 p.m. Please contact me at the Burra Police Station a.s.a.p. Reeves.'

Craig turns the key, thumping the door where it sticks in the frame. He pushes through into the house, flicking on lights. Lyn hurries after him. 'Sweetie? It must be good news. They wouldn't leave a note if it was bad.'

She sees his shapely back stiffen. He swings around to face her. Fascinated, she watches his head float down until his red eyes are level with hers. His mouth, she notices, tends to turn down at the edges, reproducing exactly his moustache.

'If it's good news, how come he didn't come out and say so? Leaving me dangling like that.'

Until Craig came along, Lyn had been the one to think negatively about everything. Bit by bit he drew her out and laughed away her fears and doubts. He saw something in her and didn't care about her past, what there was of it. But some of his huge enjoyment of life has been lost in the recent troubles and now Lyn has found herself in the position of building him up, discovering anxieties and grievances he's kept hidden all this time, all to do with his bloody family.

'There's only one way to find out. Ring.'

'What if they want me to come in for more questioning?'

For the first time, Lyn feels doubt. She feels it grip cold and tight inside her. 'Craig . . . ?'

He says stubbornly, 'Didn't do it, okay?'

'I sure hope not.'

'Thanks a lot. Bloody great. My own wife.'

Lyn pushes past him, the word 'Linny' hanging in the air behind her. The passage smells of new carpet, new paint and staleness, of air that has baked in a house shut up all day against the sun.

She's drawn to the kitchen, saving the best, the nursery, for last. She stops in the doorway, and all the disappointments of her life come swamping through her. 'Oh, no. How could you? Oh God.'

'Like I said, I been flat out. I was going to get Mum over in the morning.'

'No way. Absolutely not.'

'She won't mind.'

'It wouldn't be right. She's not young any more. She shouldn't have to clean up after us in our new house. Plus it's time you took responsibility.'

Lyn likes to keep Craig's family at arm's length. They're meddlers. They treat Craig as if he were still the baby of the family, the kid who mucked around at school, got into trouble all the time, needed looking after. Meanwhile his brothers did well, made a lot of money, got all the praise – encouraging in Craig the notion that he's dumb and hopeless and unlucky. Stuff Lyn hadn't known when she married him. Stuff she's on the way to mending in him, just as he'd mended her.

'Okay, sweetheart?'

'Okay.'

Lyn advances on the sink, pushing her sleeves to her elbows. Porridge hard as glue on her new cereal bowls, mashed potato and melted cheese caught in the tines of her forks, rings of sauce and gristly meat on every plate, gladwrap and take-away cartons on the table, old blackened spillovers around the gas burners – even a pair of overalls in the corner and a paint-brush in a saucepan of water.

Lyn looks. He's been washing brushes in the sink. She leans on the bench, head bowed, and begins to swear. It's low, fluent, bitter, intended to cut him to the bone.

After a while, she stops. Over her hammering heart she hears the beginning of an apology from her husband, low and desolate, the night and all his troubles catching up with him. But Lyn can't look at him yet. She can only go so far in propping him up. The best she can do is force some jolly encouragement into her voice:

'Enough said. I'll do the kitchen. You go and phone that policeman, then tidy our bedroom before I see it and chuck another mental, okay?'

There are a few things she wants from her wardrobe and chest of drawers. Susannah – older, calmer, more assured – always seems to stride boldly into her day at the hospital. You never saw Susannah in a dressing gown and slippers, always in bright cottons and dangly earrings, her eyes dark and flashing from a touch of make-up. That's what Lyn aspires to, a skirt-swishing approach to motherhood and life.

She hears Craig muttering on the telephone, then silence, then he's hanging uncertainly on the door frame as if asking permission to speak. Finally: 'He's not in.'

Briskly, calmly, Lyn says, 'We'll try again later. Right now, let's just get this place tidy again for when I come home, and then we can go back to the Bush and see our sweet little bub with a clear conscience.'

She senses his relief. He disappears along the passage to their bedroom. Steam rises from the sink as she sluices away tea leaves and traces of acrylic paint. She's never had hot water quite like this before, scalding hot, gushing, never running out. She tries to imagine Susannah's house and can't. She wonders if she will ever see where Susannah and Athol live. She's had to stop herself from blurting out: 'I know we'll be friends.' Maybe she will say it soon. She doesn't really know anyone here, only Craig's friends. Her own friends are over in Port Pirie. Susannah probably needs friends too, being new in the district.

Not that Lyn wants to be among her old friends again. That would be a step sideways, even back. It's always been an article of Lyn's faith to move on in life. Her mother had something to do with that, forcing her to grow up too soon. Too much self-sufficiency and knowledge too early in life can be a good thing and it can be bad. Craig could have done with more of it, Lyn thinks, and I could have done with less. Lyn is close to forgiving her mother – forgiving her for forcing her to grow up too soon, forgiving the skewiff painted mouth, orange hair, bleary eyes, poddy belly and stalk-thin arms and legs, the result of a lifetime of gin, Alpines and wrong men. Let's hope, Lyn thinks, that I never give my daughter something to forgive *me* about.

In the end, the bedroom isn't too bad. Craig is halfway through changing the sheets by the time Lyn joins him. He's already bundled his dirty clothes into the laundry basket. She flicks around the bed, tucking and smoothing. She'll have to be vigilant with him, that's all, until he unlearns what his family have taught him.

Then, so full of emotion and shyness that she can't speak and must duck her head, Lyn leads her husband along the passage to the nursery. She flicks on the light. They stand in the doorway, drinking it in, their arms around each other.

'Her little cot, her little teddies. I can't stand it.'

And her milk rushes in again. Lyn burrows her nose into the shifting flat planes of Craig's chest. He would never let anything happen to her. He's tall, angular through the torso, narrow and snaky in the hips. With any luck, Nina will have inherited his genes, and grow into someone long-legged, high-stepping, slim and flashing. Enveloped there in her husband's arms, Lyn feels better about all her flab and soreness. She'll get her shape back.

'We'd better go. I told the midwives ten o'clock.'

Outside, Craig stops to call and whistle: 'Bluff! Bluffy! Here boy!' It's a powerful, piercing, thrilling whistle, an outward sign of all his gusto and vigour. Now if Lyn can just help him go confidently into the wider world, everything will be great.

'Why don't you check our old place after you drop me at the Bush? Maybe that's where he's gone, back to his spot under the verandah.'

Craig gives it some thought. One thing, he always makes an effort to bounce back. 'Yeah. Worth a try.'

They climb into the ute. Lyn reaches for the radio switch, filling the cab with some head-banging kids' stuff. Hastily she adjusts the volume, searches for Gold 109, catches the tail end of John Lennon singing to his baby son. Delighted, she grabs Craig's arm.

'Crap.' He grins.

'Better than your crap.'

Fences, ditches, grassy culverts, road signs, pepper-trees and fences, all painted briefly in the light of their headlamps. Craig and Lyn hum past the sleeping town.

'Ten o'clock news,' Lyn says, fiddling with the volume. Two evenings ago, when she'd gone down the corridor visiting, Susannah had pointed the remote at the TV on the wall in the corner and said, 'News of the world at peace.' It stuck in Lyn's mind: the wry tone, the tone of someone who has a perspective on things. Now Lyn tries it on her tongue: 'The news of the world at peace.'

Craig's hand flashes out: 'No!'

He snaps the radio off. 'No,' he says again, more evenly this time.

Lyn understands, and feels chastened. He's sick of hearing about the murder, choice statements like 'Police are following a number of leads and anticipate making an early arrest'.

'Sorry. Didn't think.'

He rolls his shoulders.

They drive the rest of the way in silence. Now Lyn's got to recover lost ground with him. With it comes a treacherous thought: she can't wait to take her baby home tomorrow, but at the same time she's looking forward to sealing herself off from the world tonight in her room at the Bush, where everything is always all right and no one has any expectations of you.

But first she'll have to send Craig home in a happy frame of mind, or she won't be able to sleep, and Nina will pick up on all that badness in her milk and in her head. 'There's that champagne left.'

Two-thirds of a bottle of Carrington Blush, a gift from Craig's oldest brother, in the tiny bar fridge under the TV in the cabinet by the window.

'It'll be flat.'

'Still. Be a pity to waste it.'

He shrugs.

Lyn looks away, out her side window, to Dare's Hill, looming behind the town, blinking red in the night. Now their headlights are sweeping over a long, low, floodlit sign mounted on a nature strip: Pandowie Bush Nursing Hospital.

Once inside the sliding doors, Lyn begins to hurry. A baby is crying deep within the building, a thin, helpless, endless sound of heartbreak. She knows that it is Nina. Craig trails behind her like a tall, awkward boy. She comes to the glass wall of the nursery – and begins to relax. It's another poor mother's poor baby after all, somewhere down the corridor beyond the nurses' station. Nina and five other babies in the nursery, each and every one of them sleeping peacefully.

A beaming midwife appears, enveloping Lyn and her husband in the goodwill they all seem to wear here at the Bush. 'Had a nice time? Your bub's been as good as gold. We fed and changed her half an hour ago, so if you want to express now you can get in a bit of shut-eye before her next feed.'

It's Craig who wheels Nina to Lyn's room. He can't hide his pleasure in her, or in this simple act. Had he simply been scared all this time, not full of second thoughts? Lyn watches him bend and coo and chatter.

The door to Room 50 is ajar. 'Lyn? Is that you? Come and say hello.'

At once Craig makes a prohibitive, warning face at Lyn, a way of saying: 'Don't.' He's met Susannah before. He doesn't know how to behave around complicated, competent women. They scare him, and then he's liable to strike a wrong note to hide it. But Lyn is delighted. Susannah wants to see her. She mouths: 'Just a short while, Craig, okay?'

'Coming,' she calls.

And so they wheel Nina into Room 50. The radio is on, something low and classical. The blank screen of the television set glares down upon the bed like an unforgiving eye. Otherwise the room is exactly like Lyn's, only pastel blue, not pastel green. The same ensuite bathroom, double bed, TV and fridge cabinet, nursing chair, ordinary chair, baby in a bassinet under the window. Maybe fewer cards and flowers.

Athol is there. He glances up from reading a sheaf of typed pages. There is a pen in his right hand. Lyn is struck by the contrast between Susannah's husband and her own. Craig is sandy, raw and weather-reddened. His body is too big for him, a clumsy, powerful set of limbs and tendons in stretch jeans and a checked shirt. He can rarely keep still for long, rarely co-exist peacefully with himself. Athol is a cool, precise, unsmiling package of a man, and it's clear to Lyn that he doesn't want visitors. He returns to his reading. Craig's hand had shot out automatically; now it deflates, unnoticed, and Susannah says breathlessly from the bed, 'Poor Athol. Always essays to mark. So, did you have a nice time?' She pats the bed. 'Tell me about it.'

Lyn sits, talks to Susannah, half aware of her husband, the two sleeping babies, the distant, still man in the corner behind her. Craig remains standing, his head clear of the conversation swirling around the bed. After a while he's caught by an expression on Nina's face and ducks his head into the bassinet. Lyn hears a series of smooching sounds and feels flushed suddenly, giddy and elated: her baby, her husband, her new friend.

The other baby stirs. They've called him Louis. He's smaller than Nina. He frets rather more and is slow to feed. It's a drain on Susannah. It occurs to Lyn that Susannah is a little desperate tonight – for a smiling face, for company, for a respite.

They talk. Lyn, half attuned to the action of the room, hears Athol slap his pen down, hears the essays thud to the floor. He makes a business of getting out of his chair. He bends to Louis in the bassinet. Two fathers, bending over their babies.

Now Athol is drawing back the little blue bunny-rug, the hospital's over-washed nursery bedclothes, as Louis snuffles and bleats. 'My gassy little creature,' he says. 'My little creaking door.'

Yes, that's exactly right, Lyn thinks. That's exactly how Nina sounds sometimes.

Athol folds a nappy. 'We're a touch fractious, aren't we, little one. We want our nappy changed. We want some peace and quiet in our life, fresh as we are from the womb.' His hands work with cotton balls, a tube of lotion, a plastic snib. 'We want to be born of tranquil, not anxious love, don't we, little one. We don't want to take in a set of pointless fears and doubts with our mother's milk, do we, eh?' He nuzzles Louis's neck. 'Poor little tacker, stuck in a backwater. Poor little tacker, stuck in a backwater with a mother whose chief mode of expression is to fret and complain.'

Lyn immediately slides off the bed, a flush forming on her face. Susannah won't let go of her hand. Soon Susannah's thin arm is angled steeply from the banked pillows, but then the connection breaks and it falls as light and helpless as a feather to the bedspread. A wobbly smile and eyes as bright as water follow Lyn and her family out into the corridor. Lyn closes the door on her friend, on the complicated music, on the turbulent quiet in Room 50.

Back in her own room she doesn't want a cold eye looking down on her. She climbs into bed, aims the remote control, tunes the set to Channel 10, the end of 'Northern Exposure'. She's content just to let the colours and antics wash over her, the volume off.

Meanwhile Craig can't take his eyes away from Nina's little face. His soft voice is full of complicated emotions. 'We don't say nasty things to Linnie like she's not in the room, do we sweetheart? Nothing gutless like that in this family.'

He's not dumb, no matter what his family thinks. Lyn watches him dip his head, smack and smooch and tickle his moustache around Nina's sleeping ear. Then he's coming around the bed to Lyn, bending, nibbling at her lips. No, he won't have that champagne. Tip it down the sink. Give it to that arsehole next door. A sweet and fervent goodbye, a promise of tomorrow morning, when he'll come to collect her, their daughter, the cards, the flowers. He ventures gamely into the night, ready to resurrect himself, to search for his missing dog and make his phone call.

Lyn, drowsy under the covers, gazes at Nina's button mouth. On the screen there's the ten-thirty update, MANHUNT stamped over a static image of Dare's Hill, dissolving into movement, a short, overweight, shackled man being escorted by detectives sometime earlier in the day, a stretched grey cardigan hiding him from all the decent people of the world.

The Devil in Ms Jones

Leonie **Stevens**

The house is the only place with power. It's where the TV and video are, and the porn film is just getting interesting when Lorena the Earthmother bursts into the room screaming, 'I don't believe what you're doing! This is disgusting! Don't you know there're kids around?'

You peer about the room, empty but for you and Eddie – and he's only half there, giggly and fragile with the mushies taken two days ago, bloodshot eyes glued to the screen where six guys come into a skinny woman's mouth.

'Are there kids around?' you ask, though kids aren't what you're interested in. It's been five days since you finally got the cutest guy you know to travel 500 k's and a few cultural borders to visit you. It's a victory of substance over form, and you spent a couple of days introducing him to the world of tie-dyes, tofu, feral kids, tame adults, sandals, tom-toms, patchouli and rules. You've wandered through the bush, cooked fantastic meals, smoked and tripped and played scrabble by candlelight. He doesn't mind that the solar panels never heat the showers properly, and he didn't puke during the communal hug at Friday's meeting, so you figure you must be doing well.

Though not well enough. He's still sleeping on the couch in your van, always at an arm's length, but never closer. He likes you, you have to assume, because he came all this way, and you like him, you know for a fact. You see him in this world and the other, full sensory dreams of soft eyes and luminous dreads. You're convinced that he's an extraterrestrial, an entity, perfect but shy, so this morning you took decisive action. You caught a lift with Brooke to Coffs Harbour to get something from the video store. Going down was a cruise, but on the way back Brooke babbled until you were sick in the head.

'It's taken a long time,' she said, driving too fast with guarana jitters, scraping the worn underbelly of her van against the irregularity of the road. 'A lot of travel, a lot of mistakes, a lot of soul searching – not to mention pain. But now I know why we're all here.'

You braced yourself.

'It's to heal ourselves.'

You thought: heal yourself, sister, I've got 'The Devil in Miss Jones' in my backpack, and you want to say the same thing to Lorena right now, but she's screaming and the skinny woman on the screen has cum all over her mouth and there's a grudging thing called respect up here.

'Oh, lighten up,' you tell Lorena, trying to get a smile out of her thin, pinched lips. 'It's not hurting anyone.' Except maybe the woman on the screen, and she's not complaining.

'What?' Lorena roars. 'How dare you bring this smut into my space!'

You begin to feel aggrieved. A discourse on taste is one thing, but Lorena's standing over you with her hands on her hips, close-set eyes trying to burn you into submission, when all you want to do is push the yellow dreads from Eddie's face and get down to it.

'Excuse me,' you say, 'I thought this house was communal property.'

'Yeah!' Lorena screams, 'we'll see about that!', and she runs into the night to impart the news, 'Hey, there's perverts in the house!' You don't give a damn because the woman with cum on her mouth is now getting fucked in the arse and cunt, and somehow the camera gets right in for red wet hairy close-ups, and you figure she must be off her face on coke or something because she's sniffing and laughing in her hot sandwich, saying 'Yeah! Yeah!' like a joyous robot, beckoning more cocks with her tongue.

'Hey,' says Graham from the doorway, trying to pretend he's not interested in the film. He hasn't washed for many months and you can smell him from the couch. The drought is a timely excuse. 'Lorena's going nuts out there. She's getting a lynch mob together.'

You roll your eyes and say, 'This is bullshit. There's no kids around: she's the only one offended.'

Graham strokes his beard and says, 'Yeah.' And he knows what you're doing is not diabolical, but when it comes to the crunch he'll support Lorena, as will everyone else, because she's one of the original residents and no one's allowed to forget it. Great explorer Lorena, maddie's pension in hand, macheteing her way through the forest in 1976 to create a better life for those who followed.

'Listen,' Graham says, 'maybe it wouldn't be a bad idea if you –'

'Sssshhh!' Eddie snaps, eyes fast on the screen.

When Graham goes, Eddie gives you a nervous laugh, as if to say, 'This is really gross and stupid, but I'll watch the rest anyway.' And you do, together on the couch, not touching, as the close-ups of cocks and cunts and squelching noises climax in long shots of the guys coming. They pull out and dump on her pubes, and she groans like it's the ultimate high, but you wish that once – just once – you could see the woman come. You watch shaky credits until Eddie finds his voice.

'Come on,' he says, blushing, maybe breathing heavily, 'let's go for a walk.'

Walking is the last thing you want to do, but you follow him anyway, out of the communal lounge with the long leaden couches, down the hallway, past the message board where there's never anything for you, through to the kitchen where Jackie's making a stack of baked cheesecakes to sell at the market on Saturday. You figure she must have heard Lorena screaming, but she doesn't say anything, just offers you a cheesecake sample. It slides down warm like something else, and you grin at Eddie in anticipation.

The night is mild. You go through the back door, dodge the toilet and almost get snared in the jasmine before you think to turn on your torch. You've done the walk to your caravan hundreds of times in various states, but somehow, with the darkness and Lorena's rage and the joints you smoked before the video, you get lost. You know your van is just up the hill from the house, overlooking the orchard and the paddocks, but you must have veered too much this way or that, because suddenly you're in unfamiliar shadows and your torch is dulling to a Christmas-tree glow. Odd gas and kero lights permeate the shadows from other people's places, but with no moon you can't make out the difference.

'Do you know where we're going?' Eddie asks, and you snigger rather than answer and take the opportunity to grab him while he can't see your uncertainty. You find his shoulders, find his face, kiss his lips. At first it's gentle, until the video washes over. The torch falls to the ground, dead, as he starts on your clothes, and you silently curse yourself for wearing inaccessible jeans and T-shirt. Should have worn something he could tear open in one magnificent move. It's clumsy in the dark but it's happening anyway, your clothes sliding away with a sinister laugh from Eddie, until a nearby rustling that neither of you created reminds you that snakes share the property. Now, adders have their place in the erotic process. Your cousin Maureen used to do a nifty show in the Surfers strip with a carpet snake. But round here the snakes are Tigers, Browns, deadlies, and you're a city girl at heart.

'Hey,' you whisper to Eddie, 'let's go up there.' You point to the solar-powered shower block straddling the hill. 'We can find the van from there.'

He's tugging your jeans down to your knees, looking intent on doing it right here. 'Why?'

'Critters.'

You think he's taken no notice, struggling down there with your jeans, until the world spins and you realise he's lifting you up. He slings you over his shoulder so your bare arse catches the cool night breeze and carries you – you're assuming – up the hill towards the uniform square lights of the amenities block. You're almost there when you hear a gasp, and you crane your neck and see Lorena the Earthmother, upside-down, sideways, staring from the dim light of her yurt. You want to laugh.

'Caveman,' you say. 'Yeah!'

The look on her face tells you you're dead as Eddie carries you towards the light. You close your eyes, as if that will stop you being seen, and smell the washing powder. You're going through the laundry. Six super-monster-size machines, the generator and the driers that cause civil war in the wet season.

'Hi,' says a voice. Eddie puts you down and starts chatting to Brooke's boyfriend Danny while you scramble for your clothes. Danny seems a sane enough guy, and usually you wonder what he's doing with a headcase like Brooke, but tonight you're more concerned with how ridiculous you must look, clothes half up and down. Danny makes out he doesn't even notice as he forces some of his home-made firewater onto you. It's in soda water bottles and it's so explosive you could use it for molotov cocktails.

'Oh,' Eddie says, his vocal cords burnt by the drink. 'It's good!' He turns and makes you take several swigs, and your body starts shaking in rebellion, and before you know it the two of you have polished off a small bottle and Danny's picking up the empties and his washing and heading out the door.

'Oh, by the way,' he says, 'Lorena's spewin at you.'

You turn to smile at Eddie but he kisses you instead. The spirit of the video complements the firewater and you start to heat up, right there, in the laundry room. His hands are all over you and you start to worry that kids might wander in – then Lorena would really have something to gripe about – so you inch along the wall towards one of the shower cubicles. Eddie reads your mind, swings you around the corner and into the room. The wall mosaic of broken tiles and plates is rough against your skin.

'Hmmm,' he says, rubbing your tits, kissing your neck. 'Do you want to fuck?' He kisses you hard and deep because he knows the answer. Your legs curl around his waist: you want it now. 'I might fuck you,' he says, playing the game, stealing a line from somewhere in the film. 'It depends.'

Leonie Stevens

You open your mouth to say 'On what?', but he
covers it. The light in your eyes is green. He pulls up
your T-shirt and wraps it tight around your face like
a blindfold. As he guides you to the floor you think,
yes, yes, this is what I always wanted. He pulls off
your jeans and drags you across the tiles. He tears off
your bra and you lie face-down on the cold tiles as he
grabs your hands and winds the bra around them. He
bends your arms behind your back so it hurts, and it
feels so good that you forget who, what, where you
are.

'Right,' he says, taking hold of some hair through
the T-shirt that's still wrapped around your head.
'Let's go.'

You go out into the night. Occasionally he stops,
like he's watching and listening, before you move
again. Your feet leave the concrete of the shower
block and go back to dirt, stones and twigs, cutting
you, jarring your back as Eddie forces you along, one
hand clutching your hair, the other occasionally
pinching your nipples. You imagine how you must
look, naked, bound, blindfolded, stumbling through
the dark. You wish you could see yourself. You wish
someone was filming.

You descend the hill, maybe towards your caravan,
maybe anywhere. There are voices nearby and Eddie
pushes you against a tree. Lorena's telling someone,
'It's disgusting. We've got to do something about
them. It's her I blame, you know: after everything the
women's movement has achieved!'

You're pressed tit-first into a rough old tree with several fingers in your cunt.

'Look, I dunno, Lorena,' Brooke's voice says. 'I really think it's kind of up to them.'

'Not when they're using the house and the video – the COMMUNAL video – to watch that degrading filth.'

'Filth,' Eddie whispers into your ear. 'You're filth.'

That's when you know you're in for a good time. He waits for several moments until Lorena and Brooke move away, then he grabs your hair again and leads you downhill. It's rougher this time, and when you stumble and fall, he doesn't help you to your feet, he drags you. Finally the dirt beneath your feet turns to wood, and you know you're on the porch of your van.

'Right,' he says, and you hear the door open before he pushes you inside. 'Get on your knees.'

You do, in the middle of the caravan floor, listening to the sounds of Eddie fumbling around, lighting a candle, fumbling some more. He moves around, taking his time with whatever he's doing. Presently you smell dope smoke in the air, and when he lifts the T-shirt to expose your mouth you think he must be offering you a toke, but he shoves his cock in instead. He holds your head tight so you're almost gagging and keeps smoking his joint, and it's so awful and depraved that you almost come on the spot. And so does he, judging by his rigidity, until he pulls away and you hear the roach sizzle in water.

He moves around. The caravan shakes. He opens cupboards, rifles through drawers, murmuring occasionally, 'What's this? Oh, yeah!', and you figure he's found your amusements. The vibrators and lubricants and magazines that brighten a solitary existence. He picks you up by the shoulders, pushes you face-down onto the bed and starts on you with a dildo, and you feel the way you never did, like a rag doll, a simple vessel, a sex object. You're cunt and tits and mouth, that's all you are, and when he grabs you tight by the hair and forces his cock down your throat, you try to get away because you're gagging, but he fucks you even harder with the dildo till you feel yourself starting to come. He senses it and pulls everything out so you're left kneeling on the bed, hands tied, tits out, cunt throbbing.

You hear voices from outside – Lorena's caught someone else and she's telling them, 'It's disgusting. I can't believe it. This community was founded on being sexism free. I moved all the way up here to escape this kind of degrading patriarchal imagery.'

Hmmm, you think, I moved up here for the dope. Whoever Lorena's talking to murmurs and you can't identify them.

'What do you mean?' she screeches. 'Of course it's degrading! Pornography leads to rape. Everyone knows that.'

'Yeah,' Eddie whispers, suddenly close to your ear, pulling you up so your arse is in the air before he sticks the dildo in again. You're kneeling with your bum in the air and the dildo in your cunt thinking, degradation. I love it. You hear the tearing of plastic, and you know it's a condom being opened, and your head's just about exploding with anticipation when he pulls the dildo out and spreads your buttocks. About to happen. Yes.

Then he moves away again. He's teasing. He makes you kneel up straight. He pushes what smells like his T-shirt into your mouth. He ties some rope to your hands and winds it under your cunt. He ties another one around your waist and fixes the cunt one to it. He winds a belt around your tits, squashing them down. The slightest move almost sends you to orgasm.

'Jasmine!' Lorena's voice calls at the caravan up the hill. 'Are you there? I have to talk to you!'

Eddie kneels behind and starts playing you. He scrapes the belt around your tits, scratching them. He pulls the cunt rope so it cuts into you. You're almost there when he suddenly pushes you face-first into the bed and starts fucking you. The belt and the ropes are cutting in and his cock is slamming and you feel like you've died and gone to heaven. He stops for a second, spreads your legs, and you feel the tip of his cock searching out your arse. He finds your arsehole and wedges it in, just a little. Your body electrifies. He pushes it in more, spreading your thighs with his knees and going for you violently. It hurts. You try to move. He pushes your head down into the mattress so you can hardly breathe. You want to scream, no, this is not fun any more, it hurts, but he's pushing a dildo in your cunt and his hands are going for your tits. He kneads them and pinches the nipples, and the orgasm starts to come for you. It gathers strength from far away, and you try to fight it because the pain is real and you can hardly breathe, and he knows and he's saying, 'Don't you fucking come,' grabbing your tits and cunt from above, so that when you come you're in a vice, completely immobile, and you're screaming into the gag when he pulls it out and sticks his tongue in and you know he's coming too, and in that way you ride it out together. It's the fuck of your life.

When it's over, Eddie undoes some of the binds and you wriggle out of the rest. You look at each other sheepishly until the constraints are away and it's just your pure naked forms on the bed. Hair snaking, eyes smiling, Eddie touches you softly and says, 'I hope I didn't hurt you.' You smile and shake your head. This is the genuine part.

In the morning, you're in trouble. You lost the video somewhere down in the orchard, and one of Lorena's kids found it. You and Eddie go down to the house and the bosswoman's there in the kitchen with half the community. She slams the cassette on the kitchen bench.

'I suppose you're looking for this!' She's glowing, eyes sharp in victory. 'Don't think you can go watching it again, because we've taken a vote and the video's out of bounds!'

You look down the hall. There's a bolt on the lounge-room door.

'God,' you murmur. 'Save us from ourselves!'

Lorena says 'What?' The others behind her are smiling. They probably just agreed to lock up the lounge to placate her. You scoop up the video, open the case and see it's not rewound. The shop in Coffs fines you for stuff like that. You drop it in your pack and get a lift into town with Graham, who laughs and stinks the whole way. Eddie's arm is around your shoulder. You front up to the video shop, wait until the guy isn't looking, then slip the cassette in the return slot. There'll be a black mark on your computerised card, but you don't really care. It's done its job. Eddie's waiting in the pizza shop.

Pirates and Kings

Archie **Weller**

He stands upon the bare rocky shore and stares out over the choppy waves, a giant standing well over six feet. Black skin shines in the glare of the silver sun and black arrogant eyes survey this dismal, lonely place on the edge of the known world. Strange how such an empty shoreline can seem so alive with the rolling water and wheeling birds.

The wind whittles away at the trees so they are thin and spindly and not very tall. Isolated islands dot the archipelago in their hundreds. Many are mere scraps of rock, grey and worn smooth by the ocean; some are patches of arid, blindingly white sand. They are the nesting places of the Cape Barren Goose and other seabirds – and of the hundreds of seals which were the only inhabitants for thousands of years. From each island another four or five islands can be seen rising in vague misty shapes from the sea. It is an eerie and dangerous place.

Now new inhabitants have found their way here, drifting across the wide expanse of ocean to set up camp. Mostly ex-convicts or convicts on the run or adventurers seeking untamed lands. A wild bunch of men who know no law except their own rough one. They come in search of the seals that are their livelihood. They have as much respect for human life as they do for the animals they butcher with their huge clubs, staining the white sands red with blood. Sometimes it is not seal blood that soaks into the ground.

Of all this murderous crew, Black Jack Anderson is the most feared, not only because of his great strength and size. It is his overwhelming cruelty – and the brace of pistols that never leaves his side – that make him the king of this windswept, howling kingdom.

Middle Island is four miles long with a rocky coastline. Cliffs as bleak as Black Jack's scarred face rise into the hot blue or stormy grey sky. There is a good anchorage on the north of the island and here his sealing boats and huts stand. The most beautiful thing about the island is its amazing pink lagoon, formed from brine in the soil. But what eyes have these men for beauty? Many have come from the even more rugged and violent coastline of Tasmania and the Bass Strait Islands where murder and mayhem were their constant companions. Many already hold their life in forfeit, being destined for a slow death by imprisonment or a quick death by hanging when caught. What do they know of beauty or love or even friendship? All they care about is a little rum and the reluctant company of the Aboriginal girls they kidnap on a whim.

Black Jack makes an impressive figure this day in 1842 as he surveys his dying kingdom. For almost ten years he has held sway over the men who both admire and fear him. But now the seals are fewer than before and whalers are starting to come to the blossoming Albany. His nefarious activities are becoming known to the authorities and he has already been dragged before the courts on a charge of stealing. It was dismissed, but he knows he cannot live the way he desires any more. The seals are going and soon he too must go.

Perhaps he thinks of his youth spent as a slave, toiling for his white master, a cruel and savage life where death was often welcomed. Then, living as a black man in a white man's country, far from the Africa of his boyhood, how lonely he must have been, with only his superior strength to sustain him. No wonder he chose life upon the unsettled sea that cares not who a man is, killing equally white and black, pirates and kings, with its cold clammy hands and blue crooning lips.

So he came to the ends of the earth where now he can be the master, a mountain above the human flotsam that serves him. Even he must sense the irony that most of these men he beats and kicks and – sometimes – kills are the hated white men, the same race who despised and cursed him in the far-off country in which he had once dwelt on the very edge of society.

The beckoning brilliant white arms of the shore remind him of the woman Dorothy whom he lived with for a short time. Until even she could stand his temper no longer. He had rescued her from the shipwreck of the *Mountaineer* in Thistle Cove in 1835. There were a good many shipwrecks on this treacherous coast and among the submerged islands of the archipelago. Like grey, hard teeth the islands chewed up brigs, schooners, cutters, and spat the human remains out into the cold churning sea. There are some who will say not all of them were caused by nature, either, and that many of the possessions from the wrecked ships ended up in sealers' hands.

But she had been one of the survivors.

Small white hands ran over his big scarred body like seabirds running over wet sand. Silky soft white thighs wrapped around him at night, like the curling foam of the breakers. Soft words penetrated his scarred mind. He *had* loved her and she had loved him. She had travelled the long journey to Albany with him and, even after having that taste of civilisation, had come all the way back in the bucking, crowded sealers' boat. It had been her testimony that saved him from the charge of stealing; the word of a white woman that saved him from jail.

She is gone now. Back with her family who are on whaling boats and living a fine life. Sometimes her laughter echoes on the wind like a wheeling gull tossed around the grey sky. He too had laughed and smiled when she was happy. A rare time for his men to see him at ease. But he had sent away her kin – young James Newell and the youth James Manning – to take the long walk back to Albany along the empty coastline, all six hundred and fifty kilometres. Without any powder to shoot game, all they had to live on were roots and any shellfish they could find. When they arrived they were almost dead and could scarce even talk about the privations they had suffered. Were it not for some friendly Nyoongahs they met just out of town they would have died.

Perhaps that is why she left him. In any case, he is starting to lose his grasp on his power, and his tarnished crown is slipping. It was not safe for his woman to live on a solitary island with a dozen or more untrustworthy men who coveted her body, greedy and jealous for her love of the black man.

He stands on the shore, white sand stinging his arms and face. The taste of salt is in his mouth, the smell of it in his nostrils, and the jubilant wind is in his ears. How wonderful it is, he thinks, to be alive.

Lonny was too easygoing to be a really good fighter. At least that was how some people looked at it. Others just knew he was a useless drunkard who no longer had any hope or pride. Once he'd had a promising career as a boxer, with his size and speed and the bitterness in his mind that made him refuse to lie down. But boxing is a fickle game and a fair deal can sometimes be hard to find. After a few minor fights went the other way when he knew he'd won,

Lonny just wandered away. Others said the bitterness and hate had eaten into his skills like corrosive rust so he became careless and rash, losing more than he won.

Now he sat most days in the old park he called home with his friends and scattered kin, catching up on news from his drifting family. He hid his personal pain behind a cask of wine or a carton of beer with his best mate, a yellow-skinned Nyoongah called Cougar, with bright brown eyes and unruly burgundy-red hair. He was also a distant cousin of Lonny's and was a cheerful sort of drunk, pleasant to be around.

Opposite the park the flashing lights of the hotel were a lure to drag customers in off the street. The muffled rhythm of the local band oozed out the door, though the music was not for Lonny and his friends. They were not welcome there in that cosy world of backpackers and wealthy white residents who could afford the exorbitant prices the hotel charged. He had met the Samoan doorman on duty before, when the hotel reverted to being an early opener. There had been a few altercations that mostly resulted in Lonny being shoved roughly through the door to land in a heap on the street.

The park had been a meeting place for Nyoongahs even before the white man's city had crept outwards from the banks of the river and they had planted their trees here and built their pavilion for the Sunday afternoon bands to play in. So this place held special significance as a meeting and trading place for the different clans around Perth. Perhaps even Lonny's ancestors, who had come from deep down south, had travelled with their goods and stories up to this place. Certainly in the turmoil that became almost every Nyoongah's life in the early 1900s, when they were made the social outcasts of society, his family would have met up here with other family members for help and advice. For in those hard times, a lesson was firmly learnt: that you could only rely on your people. The white world, of which many Nyoongahs were at least half, had finally sold them out.

It was a fact. Lonny's grandfather had owned a block of land down by the coast and worked hard on it, turning it into his dream kingdom. But it had never truly belonged to him under the laws of the Protection Act. He could not leave it to his family. When he had developed it enough his white neighbour cheated him out of the property through devious means. When he'd tried to get justice they had sent him to Mogumber, where he tried to keep his dignity and pride in a cruel, strict, senseless place, ruled by the iron rod of Neville and his cohorts. From a man who owned property and who had been able to vote he was classified with all the other 'natives' as naughty children who were a nuisance and fit only to be servants.

Not only did they take away his grandfather's land, they split up his family as well. Lonny's mother was an intelligent quick-witted girl, who'd been deemed quite suitable as a domestic servant. She had slaved away for little pay on a station up north. She was a fair-skinned woman with hazel eyes and brown hair and she had two daughters from a white stockman there. They had wanted to marry but the Protector would not allow it. He took her two daughters from her to be educated away from the 'native camp' and she was never to see them again. But it didn't matter, this new white world said. The mother would forget about her children in a month or so, rather like a dog forgets her pups or a cat her kittens.

Of course she did not forget and she became troublesome trying to get them back. She was punished by being sent back to Mogumber where she met Djool Carpenter, a man who had been sent down from up north because he was one of the confusing 'half-castes' who didn't fit anywhere in the Aborigines Department's idea of society.

This man was to be Lonny's dad. A good, quiet man who went to war to fight for his country and earned his living clearing the country for the white man's farms. An itinerant worker always on the move with his small family. But the white people mostly looked upon them as rubbish and not humans at all. That sort of attitude can kill a man used to being proud and independent and it did kill Djool, slowly yet surely.

Many said it was the three years in a POW camp run by the ever-efficient Japanese that caused Djool to die at the early age of fifty-three. But Lonny knew Aboriginal men were bound to die ten or even twenty years earlier than their white peers simply because of the life they were forced to lead. That was one lesson he'd learnt well.

Was it any wonder then that he was bitter and full of hatred towards white people? Why he drank so much and picked fights he knew he would lose with the hulking Samoan? He had so many bad memories he did not care whether he lived or died.

They have come all the way from what, one day, the white people will call Mangles Bay. A long way from home. The reason why is because Namun has married wrongly. He is a wardong totem as is Djyap and by law they cannot marry. He must marry someone whose totem is under the wing of the white cockatoo totem. But Djyap loves this tall broad-shouldered young man whose sparse beard is already beginning to fill out. He has sharp, inquisitive, intelligent eyes and an easy laugh and he loves her, she knows. He is perhaps twenty-five years old, in the prime of his life, and she is a nubile fifteen years with the curly black hair and long lashed black eyes of her people.

Also with them on this escapade are Djyap's older sister Woluk, their young brother Goorboor and Woluk's husband, the solemn Kurgot, who is the oldest of them all at age thirty. It is he who takes them across the country of his people, the tall warlike Binjareb clan and past the land of the Ganeang over the hills to the taller copper-skinned Wilmen people to finish up in the territory of the Wudjari. They are as far south as they can go and still be in the land of the clans who speak more or less the same language and who do not practise circumcision on their young men. If they went any further east they would be in the lands of the true Desert people, amongst enemies and strange ways.

Woluk is homesick for her Bay where fish and crabs were plentiful. She misses her parents and familiar paths. But to stay there would have meant certain death for her sister, and Djyap wanted her to come so desperately. They have always been close and there could be no denying her. Her husband Kurgot had also felt the need for a journey back to see his own family and Goorboor had just come along for the adventure.

Mostly the small group has been left alone, although they get occasional curious stares from people they meet. Men and women who travel together are usually safe, unless a man from another clan fancies his chances at stealing a woman. But both Namun and Kurgot are powerfully built and even Goorboor, although not long a boy, is also tall and well built for his age. So their travels have been slow and amicable and now they are, once more, in sight of the beloved ocean. The men dream of the fish they have missed so much, which they will catch in the morning with their gidgees. The sisters keep an eye out for roots. This is all foreign territory to them and they have not yet met any Wudjari who can tell them about their country and its foods.

Another reason for departure was the meeting of the strange white ghosts who have encroached upon their homeland. While Namun and Goorboor are merely curious and wary of these pale people, Kurgot hates them with all his heart. His back still bears the scars he got when publicly flogged for taking some flour. He will never live among these cruel, unlawful men who do not live by the rules of sharing. He has also heard of the terrible massacre of his kin, the Binjareb people, and this only makes him want to get away from the white invaders as quickly and as far as he can.

They have all heard terrible accounts of mass murder on the quiet banks of the Murray River where men, women and children were blown away like leaves in the wind and all around was the dreadful sound of screaming and shooting. The men talk long and seriously into the night while the two sisters listen to the nasal murmuring and wonder if this time life is changing.

But here in the coastal lands of the Wudjari, they can almost feel at peace again, as in the times when they were as young as Goorboor is now. They have not seen a white man for some two circles of the moon and the hunting has been grand. Nights are spent in peaceful dreams or gentle loving or stories told in pleasant company. There has been no incident to mar their good luck. A pessimistic Kurgot might wonder when the bad luck a wrong marriage is sure to bring will arrive. Perhaps even on feathered silent feet with death as its brother. He likes the lively Namun and wishes no harm to befall him, but the lawmen have long memories, much patience and a long reach. Then again, there are new people and new laws upon this land now, seeping ever outwards like a poisonous wound. Perhaps the old laws will be forgotten.

Some Wilmen people they meet tell them of hordes of seals to be found off the coast, and so they come here because neither Djyap nor Goorboor have previously tasted this delicious meat. But Woluk remembers a story the Wilmen women told, of how a group in a strange land followed the advice of the people there only to find they wanted their women. In the fight that followed they all turned into stars. There they lie now, in the shape of the white man's pot that he puts upon the fire, to remind everyone to be careful of strangers.

Kurgot tugs gently at his beard and ponders. He does not really know these Wudjari and he wishes some would come and visit so he can show them his is a friendly group. It worries him that they have seen no sign of life for days.

Last night Namun came and excitedly told him that Djyap had been visited by a spirit and was with child. They are both excited by this new addition to the family. Children are special and a joy to have around. Kurgot, who is a songman among the Binjareb people, is already thinking up a song to celebrate this good news.

But still he is uneasy. As he fished last night upon the craggy shore, searching the swirling blue water for their food, he is certain he saw one of the white man's boats scuttling behind an island. But it was getting dark and there was a spray on the water forming a mist. The sense of foreboding does not leave him. Perhaps it was a ghost or perhaps a spirit of the mobarn man watching and waiting for his chance of revenge upon the laughing Namun.

Lonny called himself the King of Perth, with a faint cynical smile upon his lips. He was well-known around the streets of Perth by his contemporaries and by the police – the two groups that mattered most and featured frequently in his life. He had a reputation as an argumentative young man and his face bore the scars of numerous fights, marring his handsome looks.

He would sit like a huge spider in the crevice made by two roots of his favourite Moreton Bay Fig tree, and watch the world amble by. As long as he had his drink and his circle of friends he was happy. Who needed a home when there was a camp in amongst the trees and good company. It was how his people had lived before and how they would live again. They had never been welcome in this rushing, busy environment so they floated in the stagnant eddies of the parks, the squats, the river's edge and numerous other places where they could be left alone. That was all he wanted, which was not much – to be left alone to sit in his park and drink his drink. Every now and then he would be involved in a fight that would see him in jail for a time but he always came back to the meeting ground.

Once or twice he went down south to meet his relatives or to attend a funeral. Mostly he waited for them to come into his kingdom. It was amazing how on many a drinking session a cousin would meet a cousin (sometimes even a brother would meet a sister) neither knew existed. Then there would be tears and heartfelt hugs and laughter and another story would be tucked away, to be brought out on a colder, more miserable occasion to cheer them up.

Lonny had no such visits. His family had been small and obscure even in the Nyoongah community. He did not even look like a Nyoongah with his blue-black skin and bushy halo of hair. He did not have the comfort or protection of being able to recite names of family and so fit into the picture of Nyoongah society.

It was his dream to find his two older sisters, whom he had never seen. Or win the Lotto and look after his mum whom he rarely saw these days. The disintegration of his family had been complete.

One day – one memorable day in the grey, dull life of Lonny – a woman burst into his world. She was short and chunky with square shoulders and rolling breasts and buttocks. No one would say she was a beauty but she had a brown smooth face and wide sensual lips. If she appeared weak to anyone they had only to stare into the flashing hazel eyes glaring behind her glasses and they knew that here was a woman not to be taken lightly.

The first time Lonny saw her was when she strode across the park and began berating a group of youths enjoying a quiet beer under the trees. As he watched her get stuck into them for wasting their time drinking when their people needed all the help their young could give them, he idly thought she must be their relation. No stranger would be brave enough to walk up and talk like that. So he was surprised when, after she stalked off to another group, two of the youths staggered over to their king for advice.

'Did ya see that silly bitch? I thought she was gunna pour out Benny's drink, true's God!'

'She wouldn't bloody wanna, I'm tellin ya!' Benny said. ''Oo pressed 'er button anyways? We was just 'avin a quiet drink and mindin our own business when she gotta come bustin 'er 'ole. It's a good job I never decked 'er!'

'Don't youse know 'er, then?' Lonny said.

'Never seen 'er in me life, officer.' Cougar grinned.

'She must be one of them up-town niggers. Fuckin coconut. I'll punch 'er lights out she tries that again,' Benny growled. 'A man can't even have a quiet drink any more. Now as well as the munadj we got these Christian niggers on our necks.'

So that was the first impression the residents of the park had of Miranda. Lonny watched her carefully after that. She would harangue. She would talk quietly. She could even wheedle on occasion, but her message was always the same. It was time to leave the park and come out from the fringes of society. It was time to put the bad dreams and the drink aside and move on into the next century. Instead of killing brain cells with alcohol, enlighten them with knowledge and understanding, she urged. In the old days their ancestors used their tracking and hunting skills to fight the white man. Now education was the answer. Beat him at his own game and ride beside him, or even in front of him, into the twenty-first century. Look at Cathy Freeman, the fastest woman in the world. You too could be as proud as she is. Come into the world that has kept you out in the cold for so long and be a part of it.

'Did you know,' she said, her earnest eyes burning into the group, 'that this time last century some Nyoongahs were wealthier than wadgulas. We had money to burn because we was shearers and hunters and were the only ones doin' all the work. The wadgula would have been finished if it weren't for us. Packed up and gone home, he would have. And you know why I know all this? Because, as well as listenin to all the old fellahs, I read all the books and all the history. We was supposed to get, every year, five thousand pounds or ten per cent of the State's annual income, whichever was the largest amount. Now this State was built on sheep and wheat and gold, unna, so you can imagine all that money! Think of all the things you could do with that money!'

'Yeah, buy a Porsche!'

'Make it a re-ed one, brother!'

'I'd buy that pub across the road and let *no* white pricks in.'

'Even if they *was* wearin a tie, unna bud!' came Cougar's dry wit.

'Me, I'd get the ANC mob, or them Zulus be better. And I'd pay them to come over 'ere and blow the fuckin shit out of Perth. Like they do in Africa, ya know,' Benny growled.

'Woolah! Look out for General Benny!' his mate laughed.

'Me,' said Lonny, 'I'd just drink meself stupid, I reckon. Kinda get out of this life and all that forever.' His eyes issued a bleary challenge to the bright animated woman across the circle from him.

'The trouble is,' she said, 'that you really would do that, ay! That's all you'll be and you know yaself you could be an 'ole lot better. For ya people.'

Silence fell around the circle. No one ever answered Lonny back when he was in one of his moods.

'I got no people, girl – 'oo's your mob, anyway? Comin in bringin all these ideas into people's minds. Showin off 'ow smart you is because ya know this mob never got far in school. 'Oo are you to do all that?'

Then he got up and wandered away, his big ungainly frame melting into the blackness of the trees. The shadows blanketed him with soft rustling noise and made him feel like he belonged. Miranda stared after him for a moment then got up to go to whatever secret place she called home. No one saw her for a week after that.

The bright white face of the sun is hidden by galloping clouds as they are spurred on by the fierce winds that make the heavens their home. But down below it is hot enough for the little family to discard their kangaroo skin boakas. Woluk enjoys the harsh heat seeping into her dusky skin as she and her sister set about searching for roots.

They have found a small spring, a patch of brilliant greenery amidst this dry sandy scenery. Tomorrow, the men will go and catch a seal they can hear barking on the wind. That will be a luxury worth waiting for.

Right now they will have to settle for the roots they have collected and the unlucky kangaroo Namun has killed that day. They gather together in the middle of the day, to rest during the blistering heat.

It is at this time the visitor arrives. So silent is he that no one sees or hears him until Goorboor leaps up in fright as the man comes out on the edge of the spring. None of them have seen a black ghost before but it is certain he is not a Nyoongah. The fact that he is the tallest blackest man they have ever seen, in white man's clothes, tells them this. The strange language he drawls as he smiles around the camp confirms it. They are facing a black ghost.

Kurgot relaxes, telling the two younger men that here is a guest. A stranger, yes. But the same colour as them. What harm could he bring? Namun is more wary, pointing out the stranger walks alone and that this is a sign he has been banished from wherever he came. Goorboor returns the giant's friendly smile and tells Namun that he carries no weapons. Not even the curious stick the white men carry in their hands, that spurts fire and death even from a very long distance. Woluk and Djyap stay in one of the miahs, shy of this huge man, but he ignores them as he squats down beside the fire and accepts a piece of kangaroo meat from Kurgot.

Sharp black eyes gaze around the camp. They stare quizzically at the white ugly scars across Kurgot's back. Then he stares into Namun's wary brown eyes and wipes his hands on his old patched canvas trousers. Stands up, grinning pleasure at the meal. In one fluid movement he draws out a pistol and fires it point-blank into Kurgot's chest as he sits by the fire, his lifeless body falling into the coals. Even before the echoes of the gunshot are finished, Namun and Goorboor are running – Namun for the miah where the women and his weapons are, Goorboor for the safety of the bush.

The boy does not reach it. The second pistol shot discharges into the middle of his back and Goorboor staggers on a few more unsteady steps, arms wind-milling wildly, blood streaming from his mouth. His face is comical in its expression of surprise and pain. Then he trips and goes sprawling loosely, clumsily, dead.

Namun has taken this chance to grab a petrified Djyap. He shouts to Woluk who sits there stunned, staring with dawning horror at the corpse of her husband, burning on the fire. The giant monster is upon them, waving a wicked knife that grazes Namun's arm. He twists out of the way, pulling Djyap with him, and throws a boomerang at this evil apparition, who ducks easily and lets forth a gale of laughter. Then, with a crashing of branches, they are gone into the grey protection of the bush.

The giant turns his attention to the young woman. Hauls her up by one skinny arm as her mind awakens at his touch and she tries – too late – to escape.

She bites and kicks with both her feet and tries to scratch his face with her free arm. But he only laughs louder then smacks her across the face, sending her sprawling beside her dead man. With a grunt of pure ferocity he drags her by the hair and rubs her face in the still warm blood of Kurgot that congeals stickily on the ground. She shrieks at him and spits in his face, calling out in her language.

Good. He will enjoy taming this one. Some of the others cowed too early and he grew sick of them. He likes a feisty girl. Something he can get his teeth into. Or else he becomes bored too easily. Many a skeleton lies half buried in the drifting sand or feeds the fish at the bottom of the sea. Some he lets go, if they are favourites of his. Some, in a burst of good temper, he will give to a crewman who is loyal or who has pleased him in some way.

Heaving her kicking, squirming body up over his shoulder, he heads back towards the boat that nestles ugly and squat upon the white shore.

Everyone thought that Lonny and Miranda would be at each other forever after that first argument. He was a shy young man and at the first sign of aggression would try to escape into obscurity. But he was sullen-tempered as well and if he couldn't escape then he would hit back. So he was dangerous to cross.

Miranda would not let up. She homed in on him every time she came into the park, bringing her words and briskness with her. Benny, who once had wished to kill her, left the green shady lawns and great scarred brown trees to restart a lapsed course at TAFE. Some of the young girls took more interest in their children than their glue, after listening to her talk. Lonny clutched his cask and watched his kingdom crumble as his faithful subjects drifted away from his company. Only Cougar the court jester stuck by him.

''Oo are you to come 'ere tellin people what to do? I bet you was adopted out and lived the life of old Riley, unna. You never went to no Mission 'ome, I can tell! I bet you never knew what 'ardship was, girl!'

Her alert hazel eyes locked onto his and she said softly, 'They calls you the King of Perth, unna Lonny!'

He nodded. 'They call me Mister Perth. I know *all* the laneways. I know everybody. I got a name around 'ere,' he said proudly. It was all he had left – his name.

'They used to call our mob kings for a joke, you know,' she said gently. 'Like, put a plaque around some poor old bugger's neck with "King Billy of Geraldton" or "King Jackie of Esperance". He'd think 'e was real important. Oooh, real mooritj, 'e'd think, but all them wadgulas laughed and laughed fit to split in half. What ya reckon of *that*, King Lonny!?' she gently chiacked him.

But he walked away, shaking with rage.

For deep down he knew she spoke words of truth. All his life he had almost been there: almost been a boxer, almost done this or done that. But each time he had fallen back into apathy. And he blamed the huge billowing white world instead of himself. It was only his anger that kept him going now, and the fact that he was as human as the next person and that he did not deserve this second-rate life. It was, after all, the only one he would get. Once, he had been happy to walk from park to park, pub to pub, sometimes staying in a hostel or a squat with a woman. Ultimately, though, they both always discovered they loved the drink more than themselves and wandered off on their dizzy separate ways.

He had four children from four different girls. He never saw them though. They would probably all end up like him anyway, he thought pessimistically. Then he would see them every day in the park he called home.

A strange thing began to happen to Lonny. It became a talking point to others who resided in the park. It seemed to those who watched from their leafy bowers that Lonny started to look forward to seeing the short round figure hurrying across the park. It seemed that she now came specifically to sit and argue softly but intently with the hulking ex-boxer. They grinned among themselves and nudged each other when they saw her coming.

'If that was all she wanted she could have gone about it a quicker way.'

'Lonny don't care much for women when the love of his life sits beside 'im. Yeah, Missus Moselle, ain't it!? . . . As long as he don't fall into the arms of the white lady.'

Metho drinkers were nothing new to them, but they did not mention this out loud in Lonny's presence. It would have only caused a fight.

But fighting seemed to have faded from Lonny's mind. As the unseasonably hot summer moved into autumn and then a winter that drove the park people away like cockroaches to find warmer accommodation, Lonny also became unsettled and restless.

Now he actually spent time walking the streets with Miranda, showing her places he had lived and the stories attached to those places. The dirty old man with the raspy voice and incessant cough and jagged stump where his arm once was had been a famous shearer and a brave soldier. The sly youth with the angry eyes, quick fists and cold barren mind, who stole cars and beat up white people for fun, had the skills to be a great football player. Even the little girl staggering across the park, with her eyes glazed, voice slurred, and all around her nose yellow muck as evidence of a morning's glue sniffing, could one day write her story down or paint it on canvas for all the world to see – if she lived that long.

'If you was a real king, Lonny, you'd want your subjects to be happy, unna? You, of all that mob, could teach them something,' she said, then placed a warm hand on his arm in a moment of intimacy. 'You might be the King of Perth, bub. But me, I'm Queen of my own soul.' And he stared at her long and hard.

Namun hurries back as soon as he has hidden Djyap amongst the low spindly trees of this land. Too late! His sister-in-law is thrown by the giant into a boat, which he then pushes effortlessly off the beach out to sea. There are four dirty white men in the boat and they row while the huge black man stands and stares back at the land. Namun almost feels the man stare right through him and crouches even lower. There is nothing he can do. Tears trickle down his cheeks as he thinks of his friends Kurgot and Goorboor. But it is the woman he loves who will be more upset. After all, it is her brother lying dead and her sister who has been taken away.

Despondently he makes his way back to where Djyap sprawls weeping in the dirt. Wordlessly he packs up camp. He throws branches over his companions and wishes he could bury them properly. But he is all by himself and he wants desperately to leave this place that smells of death. No wonder they have seen no one around here. This is an evil place. It is punishment for marrying wrongly; they both know this at once. The old ones sent the black one to find them and destroy – not them, but those they loved. To let them know that laws can never be broken, even in this changing time when their white neighbours break laws every day.

As they make their lonely journey back into familiar land, Namun cannot understand what is happening to his beautiful country. Djyap is too upset to think much at all. When she does it is of the baby she carries and the hopes and fears it will experience.

This is how they cross the ranges and move into the fertile lands of the Ganeang. They tell their sad story to any they meet and get permission to hunt on the land, as they drift like a mournful wind over the country.

The cool brown waters of a river tempt them one day. While Djyap goes for a swim Namun takes his gidgee upstream to fish for the juicy perch known to frequent the well-stocked waterways. Perhaps he might catch some marron as well, he thinks, and they will have a little feast. He finds a secluded yellow sandy beach where his sharp eyes can see the fish swim by. For the first time since the murder and kidnap he is at ease.

He comes home in the middle of the day with the heat making the bush click and tick and the insects drone around him. This is the time of year when dead wood is most likely to suddenly just drop from the tree without a sound – sometimes a whole limb – and bad luck to anyone underneath. So he is extra alert as he glides towards his camp and the company of his young wife.

As he reaches the small clearing in which he left Djyap he hears the harsh language of the usurpers, the same as the one who took Woluk away. He sinks soundless to the ground, knowing without a doubt that he will not let them do the same to Djyap.

He doesn't know that the two young sons of the settler only want to talk to Djyap. They are new from England and all this world is exciting to them. Most of the natives on their father's farm are friendly and they are constantly amazed at the sight of naked females roaming about wild and free. Even to just talk with one is an adventure, although no one knows what the other says. The older one is the bolder of the

two and has got off his horse. Even now, as he
splashes water at the figure in the river, he does not
see the fear in her eyes. His thick Dorset accent calls
out eerily in the echoing space of the bush and he
laughs at the merriment of it all.

As swift and silent as one of those falling branches,
a spear whistles out of the dark bushes and thuds into
his back. His startled eyes have only a few seconds of
life left to stare astonished at the point that protrudes
from his chest. He raises his eyes to look at the girl for
a last time, then falls into the brown still river that his
father had so proudly claimed.

He does not hear his brother wheel his frightened
horse around and charge off into the bush, screaming
and yelling as though a thousand devils were after
him.

In his hurry to get out of there, Namun leaves
behind the fish he caught that day. Now . . . he knows
. . . these murderers and thieves can die just as easily
as any man. His eyes light up with a curious
brightness. He has no fear of them any more.

For the few white settlers who have pushed this far
inland there is consternation and fear. They were
given to understand that the numerous natives to be
seen were peaceful, yet it is obviously not the case. A
boy hardly eighteen years old lies dead and buried
behind his father's wooden slabbed hut. The nearest
law of any kind is the policeman in Mount Barker, or
the garrison at Kojonup who are drunk and useless
most of the time anyway.

The other Nyoongahs have felt the wrath of the white man and they have no wish to be blamed for something a stranger has done. So they are quick to tell all they know about Namun, and even offer to track him down. As well as a face there is now a name, and Namun becomes a hunted outlaw. Soon to become famous in these parts of the south-west. Nammen – or Black Bobby.

This is the life he leads for the next four years. Travelling on the run, stealing food and terrorising isolated families of farmers. He is thin and rangy from constantly being on the lookout, even from other Nyoongahs. He tells all he meets to take up arms and drive the wadgula into the sea where they came from. These are bad and dangerous people, he says, and there is still time to take back their land.

But they are worried by his fierce words and angry eyes. They are essentially a gentle people and there is plenty of land to let the few white people have a share. Kangaroos and possums are in abundance. It has been a good rainy season and the rivers are full of fish. Why bother to look for a fight, most of them ask. All remember what happened to the Binjareb people and other incidents when people started thinking about taking up arms. Besides, they argue, many are the wonderful gifts these people have brought with them: knives, axes, flour, sugar, tea, tobacco and even guns, horses and carts. Many of their young women are living with white men and they have nothing but praise for their men. The time for war is over, they say. Some wear the white man's clothes and blankets and many wear the white man's names. Even *he* is no longer Namun, but is known as Black Bobby Nammen with his woman Diana and his son they call Booyi, which is a long-necked tortoise and also his totem.

His son is Namun's only joy in these grey times. Both parents bring him up to know exactly who he is. They cannot participate in the normal tribal life because they are outcasts as well as outlaws but his father teaches him all the considerable bushlore he knows and impresses upon him the untrustworthiness of the whites. Djyap reminds him of the kidnapping of his auntie and the murder of his uncles. These things the child Booyi never forgets.

It must come to an end one day. How can one single man wage a war? It is not proven but he is thought to be the perpetrator of several lonely deaths of shepherds or settlers throughout the south. Black Bobby is a name to be feared.

It happens that while resting in the middle of the day, they are stumbled upon by a settler searching for lost sheep. This settler knows nothing about Black Bob Nammen, having just arrived in the country, but he sees a nigger on his land who is armed, so shoots him outright. He tries to shoot his gin too but she runs away. However, Namun isn't quite dead. In great pain he is bundled without ceremony into a cart, after the soldiers have all taken turns kicking this danger-ous killer around the barracks. He is taken to Perth where, without much fuss and bother, he is hung on the public gallows at the corner of Hay Street.

When Lonny the drunk now got his dole cheque he would not spend it all at once as he used to. He would wait until he saw Miranda and spend it on her, taking her to the movies or to a band. Once or twice he took her to restaurants – nothing flash, but places where he felt he fitted in. He began to buy new clothes – or as new as he could get from the Good Samaritan Industries store. He got his hair cut and began weaning himself off drink. He moved away from his old haunts and his old pals.

They did not like it, of course. They did not understand. He was their hero and now he was hardly seen. They missed his generosity with his dole cheque, as well as his able fists whenever there was trouble from outsiders. But he had left their cosy circle. He did not even have much time for his mate Cougar any more and this was seen as a betrayal. The red-headed comedian had often comforted Lonny when the world had king-hit him in the head.

The last step towards his new life came when he rented a modest flat, not too far from the park, so he could still go and see his friends. But he never told them where he lived, not even Cougar. It was great to have his own little place with a comfortable bed. The first thing he had ever truly been able to call his own – even though it was rented. But whenever the old magic of the meeting ground called out to him he would go to the dark trees and dark shady people underneath.

In all this time he did not so much as kiss Miranda, despite what his friends thought. She was more than just a girl to him. He had found his pride and, in so doing, his honour. He could once again walk tall and straight and look the world in the eye. It was all due to this short, squat girl with her untidy hair and glasses and ill-proportioned body. The girl with her sharp mind, whose sentences hit with the force of a spear.

When Woluk is brought to the island, she is almost faint with fear. The stories told to her when she was a child – about the giant Djanak, so tall he towered over the tops of trees and captured and ate wayward children – seem to have come true. The water laps hungrily at the sides of the rocking boat and she is buffeted to and fro as she huddles in the bottom. She does not dare look at the approaching island. It can only be the abode of spirits and walking dead.

She senses the men's hard eyes upon her naked, cringing form and their harsh voices wash over her like the shadows of disturbed seabirds that hover over the boat. The one who caused her all this harm stands stern and huge, ignoring her. He is as tall as the trees of the home she knows she will never see again.

When the boat scrapes against the rocky shore she is dragged roughly from the deck and hauled, screaming and fighting, off to the giant's strange miah. The raucous, lewd remarks from the other men follow her and she sees one of her kind, subdued and fearful and in a dirty pinafore, glancing at her before sliding away.

This small, windy, barren island becomes her home. She is not a willing occupant at first and Black Jack is as cruel to her as he is to everyone else. But, one day, after his version of lovemaking, she spies several white stripes across his back, similar to those on her husband's. She reasons that he, too, must have been beaten by the white men who whipped her beloved Kurgot, and she thinks how truly cruel is this race that can torture and hurt a person for no sane reason.

He sees her shy glance and the tears in her eyes. He has promised himself he will never love again after the departure of Dorothy. He shrugs his vestkin over his broad shoulders, hiding the scars of an unfair past, and glances again at her subdued face. He grunts, a pure animal noise that conveys neither understanding nor pity.

But he does not beat her as much any more and she is the only girl who really becomes his lady. She bears him a daughter and this is one child he keeps, naming her Sally Anderson after the barely remembered face of his mother, from whose skirts he was torn at the age of eleven to be sold up country. So Sally is the name of the only child he acknowledges and gives his name to.

The body of one of his crew turns up, throat slashed from ear to ear, preserved by a waterfall running into the open wound. The place hereafter is known as Dead Man's Creek and his remaining crew members are more than afraid. Perhaps the man made a remark about Black Jack's gin. Perhaps he argued over his share of money from sealing. Whatever, he was left as a clear warning that Black Jack is going over the edge of sanity. For too long he has walked these islands, whipping and beating, punching and kicking men into submission. His crew are scared into an act of bravery – or survival. Now he has so blatantly killed one of their number who can say where he will stop?

One day while Black Jack rests after the arduous task of murdering seals, someone creeps into his hut and, before he can wake up and use his lethal pistols, blows his brains out through his eye sockets.

The shot echoes across his tiny tarnished kingdom, sounding like the distant bark of the seals which brought him here to be his own master. Woluk hears it from where she plays with her daughter by the side of the pink lagoon. She stands, still and cautious. Understanding comes when she sees the crew coming over the hill towards her, grim and silent as the sands swirling around their heavy, booted feet. Even killing a man as savage as Black Jack is still called murder and most here don't want the authorities snooping around. There can be no witnesses to this act of revenge and it has been seen that he loved this woman, if only a little. She loved him too and bore his child.

There is one of all that lawless band who has a sense of kindness. As she turns to scoop up her daughter and run away she trips in her long skirt. He kills her quickly and cleanly before the others can have their fun with her. He lets no one touch the child, but takes her back to his own island where he lives with his four Aboriginal wives. They bring up the girl as one of their own and the name of Woluk is no longer mentioned. Another skeleton is sent to the ocean and a girl grows into a woman with the memory of her mother's murder as hazy as the islands she can only just see.

The rain fell down in heavy swirling torrents so the lights of the streets and buildings made watery reflections on the sleek black road and grey footpath. But not even the rain was enough to drive the people from their park. They huddled against the wall of the toilet or under the huge, quietly dripping trees.

Although it was cold and blowing a gale outside, Lonny was warm inside. For tonight was the night of his victory. He had bought a suit from a cut-price Menswear where many young up-and-coming businessmen bought their suits. It was charcoal grey and came with a free shirt, the whole lot costing two hundred dollars. He had bought a new pair of sandshoes and even a tie. After his haircut his fine-boned, handsome face could be seen, and his eyes, that had peeped out at the world, no longer hid behind bushy tangles, were no longer bleary but sharp and clear, for he drank little these days. The other part of the surprise tonight was the news that he had scored a job as a brickies labourer with another

Nyoongah tradesman who promised to teach him the skills of becoming a bricklayer.

Painted up in his white man's ochre of fine clothes and dreams of respectability he knew this would be one corroboree he'd never forget.

He had known the band playing in the pub across the road was one of Miranda's favourites, so he had invited her out on their first real date. He felt shy about it, yet proud and happy. When his friends saw him strut down the street in his suit, with his woman by his side, they would see that they too could be like him. Proud to be an Aboriginal yet striding right along in the white man's world, as good as or better than many white men. He smiled a little to himself as he saw the look on their faces. Oh yes, there would be those who accused him of going white on them, for abandoning the whispering park and its dark secret children. There would be those who'd accuse him of being a coconut, of selling out. But he still had his principles. He was still a Nyoongah on the edge of society, but he now had a flat and a job and a steady woman. The alcohol the white world had thrown his people ruined them and kept them down while they sucked what little joy there was from it. He knew this now. His mind shone as bright as a beacon and he really was a king.

When she came to the flat she didn't say anything, but he had only to look into her eyes to know she was as pleased and happy as he was. And that was how they set out. Miranda Nammen and Lonny Anderson.

The band was already playing and the place was packed when they arrived. No longer staggering or keeping to the shadows, he strode boldly up to the front, with Miranda just behind. The lights outside the entrance flickered white and brilliant red, forming a misty pool of pink light on the wet pavement. It was beautiful to see, shimmering there, and it seemed an omen of the good times ahead.

'Sorry mate. You can't come in.' The squat solid body of the Samoan stood squarely in front of him. Scornful brown eyes stared at him from a flat, scarred face.

'What do ya mean I can't come in! My money's the same as everyone else's,' Lonny said, hardly believing what he had just heard.

'You don't remember but you been barred, mate! You was too pissed to remember, ay!' the doorman said, a sneer in his voice and in his eyes.

'I 'aven't even fuckin been 'ere for ages mate!' Lonny bristled. 'Get fucked –'

Miranda placed a hand on his arm. 'Why can't we really go in, mate? Why don't you be honest with yaself and say you just doin' the wadgulas' dirty work. We used to clean up their farms for them. Now you clean up their pubs for them, unna?'

'He's not wearing the proper shoes.' The Samoan pointed to Lonny's new sandshoes. The throbbing of the music beat against the pouring rain. Miranda pointed to three Asian youths coming out of the pub.

'They're wearing sandshoes even dirtier than Lonny's, mate. What's the go there then?' she said, hands on hips.

The big man leaned close to her, ignoring Lonny. He smiled. 'Truth is, girl, he's a smart-arse troublemaker. So why don't you piss off and go where you're welcome.'

He might have said more, but, suddenly, behind Lonny and Miranda, there was a cry and a screech of brakes and a soft thud followed by a scream from the park.

Lonny turned to see Cougar stretched out on the road and one of the Asian youths getting shakily out of the car. The car had only been going ten kilometres an hour and Cougar was more shaken than hurt. Even now he was getting groggily to his feet, blood from a cut arm running with the rain.

Everything happened so fast. Afterwards no one could be sure of the exact sequence of events. Two or three of the park people had come out from the protection of the trees to see what was happening and one of the passengers got out of the car to join the driver, who was asking if Cougar was alright.

'Ya fuckin slope-head bastard. Ya can't even see, ya eyes are so fucked. Whyn't ya go back to ya own country instead of tryin to kill us all 'ere!' a female voice cried out.

The Asian youth tensed, preparing for aggression.

'Look out, 'e's goin' for Coug!'

Then a crowd came running out of the park. A bottle shattered on the road and someone threw a punch at the driver while others hustled a dazed Cougar away. Someone else kicked in a side panel of the car and then it was on.

Not everyone was involved in the fight. Most were confused about what was happening and the only identifiable enemies were the Asians, angry at the attack on their car. They went down in a mass of boots and fists, fighting all the way. But the next day it would be reported as a riot.

As soon as the fight started, Miranda ran forward shouting, 'No! No! This is not the way any more. Talk to each other, youse fellahs!'

Lonny had been on his way to check on Cougar and could only stare in dumbfounded surprise at how quickly everything happened. He stood there in shock before being shoved brutally aside. Stumbled against the wall. The doorman was pushing into the milling crowd, shoulders hunched and fists lashing out. Lonny saw the Samoan grab Miranda by the hair and twist her around, and he sprang off the wall to go and protect his woman. Then he saw something in her hand flash white in the blinking lights of the pub. Her hand seemed to caress the Samoan's brown throat.

'Shit,' he breathed. Then he was beside her, grabbing the flick-knife from her hand even as the big man fell, his feet jerking on the ground. Blood from the wound on his throat sprayed the air. The crowd scattered. Two of the Asians and a Nyoongah youth lay unconscious on the road and pavement. But the Samoan was dead.

Lonny looked into her eyes that were bright with excitement. He was scared of this girl he had thought he knew. Thinking fast he pushed her away, even though she tried to protest. 'Run! Run, girl!' he cried. He knew other Nyoongahs would find her and spirit her away. She would be safe with her own kind looking after her. If there was nothing else Nyoongahs did, they looked after their own.

For an instant she hesitated. Already the wailing of sirens was growing louder and she looked into his eyes and raised her hand. Then she was gone.

He had caught the spurt from the man's throat and his new suit was stained with blood. He called after her, 'You thought I was weak but I'll show you I'm strong. I'm the King of Perth and the blood of pirates runs in me veins. But you, you got the blood of warriors in yours and ya gotta keep up the fight the way you been doin', see Queenie!'

But it was too late for him. No one heard. Not the unconscious Asians, the crowd of frightened white people milling around the door, nor the fleeing Nyoongahs. Certainly not the dead Samoan and especially not the girl he had wished to tell that story to all along.

Four Poems

Les **Murray**

Les Murray

It Allows a Portrait in Line Scan at Fifteen

He retains a slight 'Martian' accent, from the years of
     single phrases.
He no longer hugs to disarm. It is gradually allowing
     him affection.
It does not allow proportion. Distress is absolute,
     shrieking, and runs him at frantic speed through
     crashing doors.
He likes cyborgs. Their taciturn power, with his intonation.
It still runs him around the house, alone in the dark,
     cooing and laughing.
He can read about soils, populations and New Zealand.
     On neutral topics he's illiterate.
*Arnold Schwarzenegger is an actor. He isn't a cyborg
     really, is he, Dad?*
He lives on forty acres, with animals and trees, and used
     to draw it continually.
He knows the map of Earth's fertile soils, and can draw
     it freehand.
He can only lie in a panicked shout *Sorry sorry I didn't
     do it!* warding off conflict with others and himself.
When he ran away constantly it was to the greengrocers
     to worship stacked fruit.
His favourite country was the Ukraine: it is nearly all
     deep fertile soil.
When asked to smile, he photographs a rictus-smile on
     his face.
It long forbade all naturalistic films. They were Adult
     movies.

If they (that is, he) *are bad the police will put them in hospital.*

He sometimes drew the farm amid Chinese or Balinese rice terraces.

When a runaway, he made an uproar in the police station, playing at three times adult speed.

Only animated films were proper. *Who Framed Roger Rabbit?* then authorised the rest.

Phrases spoken to him he would take as teaching and repeat.

When he worshipped fruit, he screamed as if poisoned when it was fed to him.

A one-word first conversation: *Blane – Yes! Plane, that's right, baby! – Blane.*

He has forgotten nothing, and remembers the precise quality of experiences.

It requires rulings: *Is stealing very playing up, as bad as murder?*

He counts at a glance, not looking. And he has never been lost.

When he ate only nuts and dried fruit, words were for dire emergencies.

He'd begun to talk, then returned to babble, then silence. It withdrew speech for years.

Is that very autistic, to play video games in the day?

He is anger's mirror, and magnifies any near him, raging it down.

Giggling, he crawled all over the dim Freudian psychiatrist who told us how autism results from 'refrigerator' parents.

It still won't allow him fresh fruit, or orange juice with
    bits in it.
He swam in the midwinter dam at night. It had no rules
    about cold.
He was terrified of thunder and finally cried as if in
    explanation, *It – angry!*
He grilled an egg he'd broken into bread. Exchanges of
    soil-knowledge are called landtalking.
He lives in objectivity. I was sure Bell's palsy would
    leave my face only when he said it had begun to.
Don't say word! When he was eight forbade the word
    'autistic' in his presence.
Bantering questions about girlfriends cause a terrified
    look and blocked ears.
He sometimes centred the farm in a furrowed American
    Midwest.
Eye contact, Mum! means he truly wants attention. It
    dislikes eye contact.
He is equitable and kind, and only ever a little jealous.
    It was a relief when that little arrived.
He surfs, bowls, walks for miles. For many years he
    hasn't trailed his left arm while running.
I gotta get smart! Looking terrified into the years. *I
    gotta get smart!*

Under the Banana Mountains

At the edge of the tropics
they cut on the hills
raw shapes of other hills
and colour them banana.
One I used to see towering
each time I came away
climbed up and up, dressed in
a banana-tree beach shirt
with bush around its shoulders
like thrown-back jersey sleeves
and the rimmed sea below
drawing real estate to it.
Two islands were named Solitary
and the town wharf was crumbling
but surfers climbed sea-faces
on their boards, hand over hand.
The perched banana farms
mounted thousandfold stands
of room-long Chinese banners
or green to yellow lash-ups
of quill pens, splitting-edged,
their ink points in scrap vellum
each time I came away,
shiplapped fruit in blue mantles
all gaslit by the sun
and men drove tractors sidelong
like fighter planes, round steeps
worse than killed Grace Kelly.

Their scale came down to us
or caught around high-set houses.
I had shining hospitality
in dimmed subtropic rooms,
I unveiled a pastel school
and swift days keep passing
since I came away.

Australian Love Poem
for Jennifer Strauss

A primary teacher taking courses,
he loved the little girls,
never hard enough to be sacked:
parents made him change schools.

When sure this was his life sentence,
he dropped studies for routine:
the job, the Turf papers, beer,
the then-new poker machine.

Always urbane, he boarded happily
among show-jump ribbons, nailed towels,
stockwhip attitudes he'd find reasons for
and a paddock view, with fowls.

Because the old days weren't connected
the boss wouldn't have the phone.
The wife loved cards, outings, Danny Boy,
sweet malice in a mourning tone.

Life had set his hosts aside, as a couple,
from verve or parenthood.
How they lived as a threesome enlivened them
and need not be understood.

Euchre hands that brushed away the decades
also fanned rumour
and mothers of daughters banned the teacher
in his raceday humour,

but snap brim feigning awe of fat-cattle brim
and the henna rinse between them
enlarged each of the three to the others, till
the boss fell on his farm.

Alone together then, beyond the talk,
he'd cook, and tint, and curl,
and sit voluble through rare family visits
to his dazed little girl.

As she got lost in the years
where she would wander,
her boy would hold her in bed
and wash sheets to spread under.

But when her relations carried her,
murmuring, out to their van,
he fled that day, as one with no rights,
as an unthanked old man.

Inside Ayers Rock

Inside Ayers Rock is lit
with paired fluorescent lights
on steel pillars supporting the ceiling
of haze-blue marquee cloth
high above the non-slip pavers.
Curving around the cafeteria
throughout vast inner space
is a Milky Way of plastic chairs
in foursomes around tables
all the way to the truck drivers' enclave.
Dusted coolabah trees grow to the ceiling,
TVs talk in gassy colours, and
round the walls are Outback shop fronts:
the Beehive Bookshop for brochures,
Casual Clobber, the bottled Country Kitchen
and the sheet-iron Dreamtime Experience
that is turned off at night.
A high bank of medal-ribbony
lolly jars presides over
island counters like opened crates,
one labelled White Mugs, and covered with them.
A two-dimensional policeman
discourages shoplifting of gifts
and near the entrance, where you pay
for fuel, there stands a tribal man
in rib-paint and pubic tassel.
It is all gentle and kind.

Les Murray

In beyond the children's playworld
there are fossils, like crumpled
old drawings of creatures in rock.

Just Us

Zyta **Plavic**

My son Ben is sitting opposite me with my mother and father. They are not permitted to sit next to me – there is a table between us. Ben is three and a half years old, and not used to seeing me dressed in white overalls. A prison officer stands two metres away, watching us, listening to our conversation. This is normal procedure for visits at Mulawa Correctional Centre.

We all just look at each other.

'How are you Ben?' I ask.

He looks at me. He can't understand what's going on and is intimidated by the surroundings. No one knows what to say, or how to behave.

'Are you alright? How do they treat you here?' My mother's voice interrupts the silence. She looks like a typical cuddly, New-Australian-Wog. Her eyes are bloodshot from crying. God, I love her.

'I'm alright. It's strange, but I'm alright.'

'Tell me, what are the people like?' she persists. 'What sort of food do you get?'

'It's alright, Mum. We have buy-ups once a week when we can buy extra food.'

'Do you need some money?' my father says as he pulls out twenty dollars from his top pocket.

'No Dad, you can't give me money like that –'

'Hey, what are you doing?' the prison officer shouts, moving in to stand over my father. 'Your visit is terminated for passing contraband to a prisoner.'

'I didn't know,' my father replies. He is so apologetic, I feel like crying. The love of good parents. They will fight, or be humble, to help their child.

Our visit is terminated.

'Male in the wing,' filters into my cell, accompanied by key rattling sound effects. Cell doors are unlocked with the parrot phrase 'Morning'. The prisoner's name is sometimes added to give the illusion of a human touch. The prisoner must respond so the screw knows the prisoner is still alive. A death in custody is serious – it means extra paper work. My door opens, a male peers in at me: 'Morning Zyta.'

'Morning,' I quickly reply. He goes to the next cell for a peep at another woman in bed.

'Muster,' echoes through my cell. I jump out of bed, and frantically pull on yesterday's clothes. The pressure begins. Muster in theory is at seven a.m. In reality these Kamikaze raids can occur any time from quarter-to-seven to quarter-to-eight, and if you're not immediately out of your cell, fully dressed, you get charged and punished. Getting punished is no big deal, but charges stay on prisoners' jail records, and are used by Corrective Services and Parole as weapons against the prisoner. I make it out into the recreation area, and stand in front of my cell door. Each inmate replies to her name as it is called. After all, some cunning criminal might have escaped since the cell doors were unlocked five minutes ago.

I return to my room, and have a shower – the water leaks, and splashes everywhere. How many people ripped the taxpayers off when this prison was built? The buildings are lemons.

Drying myself I wonder what to wear. Green, or green? Will I wear the track pants with the hole in the knee, or the ones with the hole in the arse? I gave up trying to get my torn clothes replaced over six months ago. It's freezing outside – shorts are out of the question. I put on my holey green T-shirt, paper-thin sloppy-joe, old ripped socks and eroded Dunlop Volley shoes. I'll be wet by the time I get to work. Raincoats and jackets are a privilege in this prison. I console myself with a pig-out on bread before they kick me out of the wing.

Today is buy-up day, the one day of the week when prisoners can purchase necessary toiletries, and extra food stuffs. I wait in a line in front of the canteen window for fifteen minutes to be told that I have no money in my account for a buy-up.

'But I get paid thirteen dollars every week.'

'It's not our fault. Next.'

This is the second week I've had no money for a buy-up. I can't even afford to pay the fifty cent fee to get a print-out of my account.

Church service is over. I catch up on grapevine gossip. Tracey is a 22-year-old, dark-haired beauty – sweet and petite – who uses heroin and enjoys prescription barbiturates. In prison she indulges in an open medical invitation to expand and complement her drug-taking with a choice of psychiatric medications.

Tracey is your prison stereotype. Sexually abused by her older brother throughout her childhood, when she discovered he had also been preying on their six-year-old sister, she told her parents. Her father went to his youngest daughter with a belt in his hand and, seething with rage, demanded to know if his son was guilty. Terrified, the child said: 'No.' From then on, Tracey began running away from home, and was subsequently labelled uncontrollable. She became a State Ward.

I watch her sway before me, pilled-out, her eyes blank. Her speech is slow. 'Jean slashed up after lock-in. They came and got her around midnight.'

'How many is that for the week?' I hide my envy of these women who dare to feel, and have the courage to call for help. If you're feeling suicidal around here you've got to kill yourself to prove it. 'How did you do at court on Friday?'

'Ten months for all my charges. The judge said the police were egging me on because I was filling their orders for hot gear every time I went to their fucking undercover hock shop.'

'You've been in here nearly that long. You did alright.'

'You think so? My boyfriend got bail when they busted him. Then, when he went for sentencing two weeks ago, he got rehab. He comes from a very respectable family, in case you didn't guess. Anyway, when I get out this time, I'm not coming back.'

In prison people come and go at a constant rate, but some of us do not. I say my farewell and we scatter to the different locations where we are each held. It's an autumn Sunday. I walk alone along the asphalt. A Willie wagtail swoops ahead, lands to give me a quick tail-feather shake, then darts out of sight.

My stroll is stopped by an overly familiar thirty-foot-high fence. 'Officer,' I yell into the air. A prison officer appears on the other side. She is one of those screws who make my blood go cold: a disturbed woman with a drinking problem who takes delight in pushing prisoners to the point where they would hit her in despair.

'Pass!' she demands with authority. I obey by handing her a little blue piece of paper. It conveys that I had attended the church service at nine-fifteen a.m. She reciprocates by unlocking a padlock and then opening a gate that is nestled in the monstrous fence. I walk through to be stopped by the gate master's voice, 'Wait here.' Her hands professionally tangle with lock and key.

The gate master stands in front of me with a smirk on her troll face. I sense danger. 'This is a pat-down. Empty your pockets.' I have a pen in my pocket that I had smoked marijuana through. I pull out a handkerchief, and the pen. She zooms in, eyes sparkling, like a dog that has just found a bone.

The deputy superintendent, Mrs Clayton, miraculously appears on the other side of the gate where I'd been ninety seconds ago. She blurts out, 'I saw you take something from another prisoner and put it in your pocket.' She had watched me talking to Tracey, with whom she had personal scores to settle. She must have radioed ahead for me to be searched.

I have been in prison on remand for twenty-two months awaiting trial. I'd had a few smokes of hemp to help me cope with my fear of soon being in a courtroom with members of the police force, who were the most dangerous and dishonest human beings I've ever met.

I could have used the legitimate coping methods. The sleeping pills, methadone, or psychiatric medication offered by the system, but I had stopped using methadone six months ago. Now I was to be punished for not using the system's answer to mental health.

The gate master takes me to the deputy superintendent's office, where she adheres to Mulawa protocol. 'You're tipped, and I order you to be taken to the Annexe for a target urine.' The implications of this statement are many. I would be sent to a part of the prison with worse living conditions, automatically sacked from my job, and only allowed ten-dollar weekly buy-ups for a month. For the next three months I'd be on non-contact box visits, and I could not apply for work in the prison for twenty-eight days. When the target urine eventually returns to Mulawa I would be given all the same punishments again, except I'd get six months of box visits next time, because it will be my second drug charge in prison.

An officer is called to escort me to the Annexe. The Annexe is the Health Department's interpretation of a medical centre for female inmates. Upon entering I am placed in a small, dirty room while the escorting officer has a cup of coffee. I wait and listen to male officers talking about their sexual encounters.

'She had the best tits I've ever seen.'

'Did ya fuck her?'

'What do you reckon?'

Two boys who still have their lunches cut at home. At work they can dominate all the women they want. Half an hour of being subjected to their sexual fantasies is torture.

'What's going on out there?' I call out.

'The female officers are busy, you'll have to wait.'

I wait and listen to the antics of young boys for another hour. Finally a female officer takes me to the Annexe prisoners' toilet where we join another female officer.

'This is a target urine. You will be charged for refusing a urine if you do not comply. You must fill the plastic jar mid-stream, or you will be charged for refusing to supply. I'll search you first.' I am patted down, pockets emptied, and then made to wash my hands. 'You can go now.'

I pull my pants down, and sit on the toilet. Two pairs of eyes peer at me. My piss hits the water. I stop. One officer passes me a plastic jar with her gloved hand, and I fill it to the brim, and pass it to her. Cop this you straight bastards, may you get run over by a truck on the way home. She takes it from me gingerly. I pull my pants back up, and am told I can wash my hands now. The three of us leave the toilet, and I am ordered to sign a number of papers to make the valuable piss-in-the-jar all above board for future lynchings.

The day closes with me sitting in Conlon, a building where new arrivals are taken and also where prisoners are sent as punishment. This will be home for the next three months.

A few days later I am called to the Conlon fence by Karen, a plump and effervescent friend, eager to tell me some news. She came to Mulawa a few days before me, and got two-and-a-half years for accepting a parcel of 350 grams of heroin from overseas.

'You know how you got tipped for that pen? The same screw found one in Sandra's room. She never got charged, or urined, or nothin.'

'That's typical. The only thing that's consistent in here is the fence.'

'I knew she was a dog. They know she gets drops on her visits – they even let her get them.'

'That's the way it is.'

'Suck cock and arse, and help them set people up, and you can do whatever you want. You should appeal.'

'Get real. They can do whatever they want.'

'Ain't that a fact.'

I am having a legal visit with my solicitor. We are discussing six tapes the police submitted as evidence of my crime – recordings of supposed conversations between me and an undercover agent of the constabulary. I have spent the last few weeks trying to decipher them. Even with the written transcripts they are impossible to follow. The tapes played noise with scattered phrases that could be heard at just the right intervals to support a drug conspiracy. Thirty Drug Enforcement Agency (DEA) officers have spent three months to arrest one junkie on a methadone program, and now the Department of Public Prosecutions (DPP) is preparing a case against me on the basis of the DEA infiltrating a major drug importing crime ring. In Australia anyone can be charged with conspiracy from a conversation or action that constitutes intention to break the law.

James Cullen could have been a banker. He was sixty years old and totally bald. He asked me if I wanted to buy one ounce of heroin. To me it was an opportunity to use heroin for six months and not have my life ruled by chasing it. But then things started to get complicated.

Cullen introduced me to his partner, Michael Dyson, a six-foot-tall gangster type with curly, shoulder-length, greased hair. Together they made me a number of propositions that became more confusing as the weeks went by. Cullen wanted me to go overseas and do a drug run, but I wasn't interested. Next, Dyson asked me if I would go overseas with him to ensure he had access to help, in case he got into trouble with the law. I was like an alcoholic chasing that next drink. I was hooked, but I had a son to look after, and I was already on bail for trumped-up DEA charges.

I approached Tom, a friend of a friend, who enjoyed travelling and worked as a trades person. Every few years he would indulge himself with an overseas trip. I told him about Cullen and Dyson, and said he could get a free holiday out of the whole deal. Tom was interested so I said I'd arrange a meeting.

We all met over a few drinks on the ninth of May. After that meeting we never saw Cullen again. Dyson told us he'd been taken to hospital with a kidney infection. The weeks passed, and Dyson liaised between all the insects in his web. He told us his deadline was the twenty-first of May because he had paid off a particular boat captain.

Around this time I got a telephone call. 'This is Detective Stark from the DEA.'

'Yes?'

'We have seven thousand dollars that was confiscated from your husband. We are releasing it to you on his behalf. Could you come to the Sydney Police Centre near Central Station to pick it up?'

'Yeh, alright. When?'

'Wednesday three o'clock.'

That was a strange phone call. My husband, Tony, was arrested for breaking bail conditions at the airport while attempting to leave the country with another woman. He was on a false passport that Cullen had arranged for him. On his arrest, DEA officers discovered seven thousand dollars on his person which they confiscated. Five months later he was still in prison on remand, and they telephoned me out of the blue to pick up his money.

Detective Stark gave me seven thousand dollars, and a week later Dyson wanted two thousand dollars in advance on the ounce of heroin Cullen and I had originally agreed upon. I gave Dyson two thousand dollars and said I would pay the rest when he had the dope. Dyson agreed and took the money. Dyson then contacted me a few days later, telling me the deal was off if I did not pay him all the money in advance.

When I gave Dyson the other five thousand dollars and watched him walk away, I asked myself what the fuck I was doing. He phoned me at ten that same night and said we needed to meet. We agreed on the Piccolo Bar in Kings Cross. I realised I was being manipulated by him and that things had gotten out of hand. I'd decided I didn't want to have anything more to do with Dyson and I wanted my money back, but I was afraid of how he'd react. I arrived late for the meeting and dropped the bombshell. 'I don't want to be involved in this and I want my money back.' He agreed to give me back my money, but then tried to talk me around to his way of thinking by using a combination of threats and nice guy scenarios. I was grateful to part company.

The next day he phoned me to arrange a meeting time and place. We agreed on Thursday the sixteenth at a coffee shop in Leichhardt. Before this I arranged a meeting with Tom and told him how I'd handed over seven thousand dollars to Dyson but now I wanted my money back. We decided that together we would tell him we wanted no part of his plans.

Dyson was surprised to see Tom with me. The greeting formalities taken care of, I asked him, 'Do you have my money?'

Dyson yelled, 'I'm not going to be fucked around.' Then he kept talking and planning, like a madman. We told him we wanted nothing to do with the deal and left the coffee shop, but when we split Dyson followed Tom.

Instead of returning home I stayed at a friend's place so I couldn't be contacted. I'd given up on getting my money back. I feared Dyson was either planning to rip me off, or was setting me up to get busted – I had been a junkie long enough to know that setting drug addicts up to take dummy busts, as part of a business arrangement with police, ensures financial success in the black-market drug trade and no convictions.

I learnt later that both Cullen and Dyson were leaving phone messages for me at home, and that Dyson had given Tom two aeroplane tickets and two thousand dollars. Tom and his girlfriend, Pam, were to change the ticket dates for the twenty-first of May, too late for Dyson's deadline. All they wanted was a free holiday in Thailand, but they were in for a big surprise. When they turned up at Sydney Airport, Dyson appeared out of thin air. And he was still scheming. This time he was planning how he could meet Tom in Bangkok.

'What have you got to say about the tapes?' My solicitor's question brings me back to the present. 'Did you mark where they'd been cut so that when I send them out to be analysed they know where to look?'

'I didn't know where to mark the tape transcriptions because they've been tampered with every few words. Dyson's saying things I never heard him say before. On one of the tapes he says everything's got to be done by the thirty-first, but the deadline he gave was the twenty-first. Three of the tapes with my voice are dated after I went and hid at a friend's place.'

'Alright. This week I'm sending the tapes out to an acoustics laboratory. I'll let you know what they find.'

Weeks pass. I receive a letter from my solicitor, and with it is a letter from an acoustics company. I'm informed that they could not prove the tapes had been tampered with. My faith and hope in justice is now to be kept alive by a life-support machine called a jury.

I hear the rattle of keys and my cell door is opened. An officer calls from the doorway, 'We'll be back to pick you up in half an hour.' My cell door is locked again.

I have been going to the Downing Centre in the city, with its maze of courtrooms and cells, for two weeks now, and am familiar with the routine. It is four a.m. and by four-thirty I will be in a three-metre-square holding cell at Mulawa with a toilet and maybe as many as fifteen other women also waiting for transport to go to court.

'What time is it?' I ask anyone in the cell who has a watch.

'Seven-twenty.'

There are twelve of us today. We are a mixed bunch, all dressed in civilian clothes, except for two girls who do not have family or friends to bring any in. We each have a story to tell, and I have heard many in the previous two weeks. Some women need help, but are jailed instead. Most are drug addicts.

We're all going to a crap shoot. Some of us will return with prison sentences, others will get bail, some will win appeals, others will lose them, and some will go to mentions a few more times before they are genuinely heard in a court of law.

We hear a truck pull in. It's too early to be my transport.

'Where's everyone going? I'm going to Liverpool,' one woman calls out.

'I'm going to Sutherland Local. We'll be on the same meat truck.'

Five minutes later an officer unlocks the cell and calls the two women out. Ten of us are left. Finally another truck arrives. We each sign warrants to attend court, and are searched and handcuffed: after a four and a half hour process since being woken up, we are on our way.

We are cramped. We wear no seat-belts, and breathe in the sour smell of vomit mixed with cigarette smoke, trapped in traffic with a driver from hell. We smoke. There's as much hope as there is air as we are thrown around the cabin.

Ten a.m. the truck pulls into the Downing Centre. I am rushed to a basement cell, strip searched, and taken to a lift. The court officers put me in a toilet next to the courtroom, while they inform the judge in his chambers that I have arrived.

Eventually I am taken into the courtroom. It is packed. I am seated in the dock with my co-accused, Tom, and his girlfriend, Pam. Pam had been in Mulawa for six months before obtaining a reasonable bail. Tom had had bail refused. Like myself. He was kept in custody at Parramatta Prison. The three of us are having a joint trial at the insistence of the prosecution.

The prosecutor is a woman with heavy-duty luggage under her eyes and a hook nose. She has two assistants: a puppy trying to be a Bull Terrier, and a woman built like a brick shit-house. Next to the prosecutor are three barristers, each with a solicitor. One pair for each of us. Two women sit in front of the judge's bench. One is the court stenographer and the other is his show piece, a pretty young schoolgirl type who passes papers to the judge and smiles – her life-threatening problems are what her make-up looks like, and what dress she'll buy today.

The bailiff stands in front of the judge's bench and calls, 'All rise. Court now in session.' My trial is to begin at last. The judge enters the courtroom wearing a yellow stained wig and black robe with a red and mauve sash around his neck. He walks ceremoniously to his throne. After two years on remand all I can think of is how can I expect justice in this sort of environment.

After the pomp and ceremony I am taken back to the bowels of the court for lunch. I know the food routine. Two sandwiches from a public cafeteria, one apple, and one cup of coffee – my most appetising meal of the day. Breakfast was a cup of coffee. I am living on vitamin pills I have purchased through the jail.

I enter a cell and join six other women. One woman uses the communal toilet without any privacy, the rest of us talk amongst ourselves in an attempt to create the impression no one is noticing. Our lunches come. They do not get much interest, and are left with the packets ripped open as we zombie around the cell benches.

'What do you do in here if you get your periods?' The speaker is so uncomfortable she has waited half an hour after going to the toilet before she asks.

'Press the alarm, when the screw comes, get 'em to get you something.'

The woman begins crying. Another woman gets up and presses the alarm. 'What do you use, love: plugs or surfboards?'

Five minutes later a male screw comes to the cell door. 'Who pressed the alarm?'

One woman replies, 'Someone's got their periods, can you get some tampons?'

'Alright.' And he leaves.

Eventually he returns with a female officer. She looks in through the perspex viewing glass and calls, 'Who's got their periods?' All the time in jail I have done does not save me from feeling for this woman.

Keys rattle the cell door open. 'Plavic. Upstairs.'

By the end of the day the jury are sworn in – six attractive young women, five young men and one middle-aged Asian male. I am taken back to the basement and wait two hours for transport back to Mulawa.

The next day the prosecutor opens the trial with the Crown's argument as to why I and my co-accused are guilty of conspiring to import a trafficable quantity of heroin. I wonder if she believes what she is saying or if she is so professional that she could be paid to say and believe anything.

'Zyta Plavic has tentacles all over Asia!' I do not know any Asians, nor have I been to Asia, but these are the colourful phrases she uses, and the type of unsubstantiated claims she makes. The court loves it. Her argument continues with the submitting of exhibits to the court: plane tickets, six tapes, transcriptions of the tapes, statements made by the police, and money. That night I say to my cell mate, 'They're going to find me guilty.'

Dyson spends many days in the witness box, answering questions and reading from his personal statements. The defence is denied access to any running sheets – the records of the investigation – the prosecutor saying they were lost, and that the paper work they did have would compromise current police investigations.

The days pass like the turning of a torture rack. I do not have a thing in common with anyone in the courtroom. From unwilling participant, I transcend to curious court observer. I see each person's demons, I do not condone their behaviour – I feel enlightened with a strange kind of gratitude at being detached from them all.

Shpeck, Muldone, Stark, Richards, Locky, Kowman and still more law enforcers come swearing to tell the truth, the whole truth and nothing but the truth. The jury has written transcripts of the tapes and they know the tapes are real because the police said so. The facts are in front of them in black and white, and the DPP did say 'Zyta Plavic is a liar'. The almost completely inaudible quality of the taped evidence is blamed on faulty taping equipment.

A glimmer of hope: my barrister brings to the court's attention the fact that the date on the tickets used does not correspond with the DPP's evidence. The next day the judge is given a medical certificate stating that the travel agent involved has had a stroke and cannot remember anything. Dyson then informs the jury that the travel agent had simply made a mistake.

Seven weeks of insanity and the jury are about to give their verdict. Pam: not guilty. Tom: a hung jury. And me – guilty.

A few days pass and I stand before my trial judge for sentencing. 'Ms Plavic is guilty beyond reasonable doubt of conspiracy to import no less than 350 grams of heroin from Thailand. The maximum penalty for the offence is twenty years. I take into account the fact that no contrition has been demonstrated by a plea of guilty. I express condolences that Ms Plavic's son will not have a mother for many more years, and subsequently sentence Ms Plavic to nine years with consideration for parole after a minimum of six.' His words float past my ears, reality drowning in disbelief. I am escorted from the courtroom. I recall Detective Shpeck once boasting to me that jurors are idiots and believe whatever the police tell them. A junkie goes to prison and the police celebrate another victory with alcohol.

I sit in a locked room the size of a telephone box, dressed in white overalls. I'm still on three months of no contact visits. My husband is opposite me. He is a small, balding man – thin and ordinary. It certainly wasn't his looks that got us together – more like heroin and heaps of charm. We are kept apart by perspex glass, metal and wood. 'I can't believe you got found guilty,' he says.

'It's all over Tony, they ate me alive.'

'You'll win your appeal.'

'I just got a letter from Legal Aid refusing to fund my appeal.'

'We'll get a private solicitor.'

'With what money?'

He begins to cry. I wish he would disappear. Having feelings is not the way to survive in jail. I am no longer the person he knew.

I leave my visitor, and return to the familiar isolation of prison life. Two officers strip search me, then tell me to dress into my prison clothes. As I leave the visiting area I see Tracey.

'You're back . . .' She had only been released ten days ago.

'Yeh.' Tears come to her eyes. We embrace tightly.

'Hey, you two! Get going. Now!' a homophobic prison officer yells.

'Fuck off you son of a slut,' Tracey replies, pilled-out as usual.

'Go now or you'll both be charged.' The officer begins walking towards us.

We let go. 'You put yourselves in here.' He can't restrain himself.

Mid-afternoon, and I return to the location where I am housed. I walk into a prison cell. It is a bathroom with a bed in it. My home and refuge. I observe that all my possessions have been moved in yet another cell search. 'Mongrel fucking screws,' I say to myself. I get up to see if they've taken anything from my cell this time. Upon investigation I realise an almost full bottle of vitamin tablets has been emptied except for six lone vitamin pills. Prisoners are allowed six over-the-counter tablets for medication purposes.

I approach a prison officer and assume the identity of a polite little girl who is grateful for their attention. 'Excuse me, can you please have a look in the Search Book to see if anything has been taken from my room today?' He puts his magazine down and looks at me. I hate this screw – something about him – he is so pathetic. Finally he reaches for the book, slowly opens it, and finds the right page. 'You had excess medication taken from your room today.'

'It was vitamin pills that I bought on my buy-up. How can I get them back?'

'I don't know,' and yawning, he closes the Search Book.

'I should know better,' I think to myself, and return to my cell. I lie down. My eyes close, I retreat to the sanctuary of sleep.

'Who took my milk?' I hear.

'When are they going to send us some clothes washing detergent? We haven't had any for weeks.'

My eyes open. Don't these fucking bitches have any consideration for anyone who's asleep?

'Muster!' a screw calls out. I jump up, put on my shoes, exit my cell, and stand outside my door. Another screw begins calling out prisoners' names. 'Karen, this is a formal muster, go and put on your shoes.' The screw waits for her to get shoes, and we all wait for the screw. Muster begins from the start again despite two prisoners washing dishes and another two prisoners simply poking their heads around their cell doors when they hear their names called.

Muster over, I knock on Karen's cell door. 'Come in.' She's going home tomorrow.

'How's it feel, are you nervous?'

'I can't wait, I don't think I'll get any sleep tonight.'

'What's the first thing you're going to do when you get out?'

Karen looks at me. 'Have a hit of some really good smack.'

The prison permits me to have one seven-minute phone call a week. I phone my son on average about once a month. He has a life out there – to a child of six I am a voice from the dead, a wandering spirit. My mother regularly visits, and keeps throwing naive lines of hope. She tells me my son needs to hear my voice and makes me promise to ring Ben more often. Ben lives 500 kilometres from Sydney, with his father, stepmother, five stepsisters and a half-brother or sister on the way.

'Is Tony Plavic there? . . . This is an officer from Mulawa Women's Training and Correctional Centre, do you want to accept a call from Zyta Plavic? . . . I'm informing you that this call may be monitored.' The officer passes the receiver to me. I have a polite conversation with Tony and then he puts Ben on.

'Hi darling, how are you?'

'Good.'

'What have you been doing?'

'Nothing.'

'How's school going?'

'I miss you, Mum.'

'I miss you too, Ben.'

'When are you going to get out of prison?'

'In three years.'

Silence, and then he says, 'I love you, Mum.'

A painfully long siren warns it is six-thirty a.m. I open my eyes with my first habitual thought, 'Not another fucking day.' I lie in bed. I curse the world. Depression has been with me for months. After six years in prison no one's going to give me a job – even government departments by law can't employ anyone with a criminal record. After my stint behind bars all I've got to look forward to is more jail, or if I'm lucky, some dope, the dole and prostitution. After all the strip searches I've gone through, I may as well get some money for it.

I hear the excruciatingly painful rattle of keys. I fantasise about murder, determined I'm not going to be just another prison suicide or mutilation statistic. The only thing about the screws you can count on is that they walk around with their keys like babies with rattles. I want to kill all of them. What sort of death do they deserve? Their heads cut off and stuck in a toilet bowl with mouths open so that everyone can shit into them. The rest of the body parts could be dispersed around the prison to feed the crows. I am feeling better. I just might get through another day.

Barring Down

James **McQueen**

At first, when the clamour of the telephone pulled me from sleep, I couldn't tell whether the faint hands of the bedside clock pointed to two o'clock or ten past twelve. In the living-room the darkness was less dense; there was a thin wash of cold light from the street lamp outside the window. Two o'clock it was. I might have guessed. It always seemed to happen on the night shift. I wondered briefly which poor bugger was in trouble this time, and picked up the phone to find out.

The security officer didn't tell me much. Didn't know much. Just that it was underground, and bad.

I hung up, found a clean pair of socks, yesterday's clothes. A thick jumper, a windcheater. Gwen had turned over and gone back to sleep. A splash of freezing water, a quick comb. Cigarettes, lighter, torch, car keys. A quick glance in the boys' room. Both sleeping soundly.

Outside it was cold. Clouds were sailing fast overhead, driven by a gusty wind. Sickly moonlight flooding through the breaks. The street was deserted, the houses closed and dark. The car started sluggishly.

As I swung into Howard's driveway the headlights caught his figure by the door where he was waiting, sweater and trousers pulled on over pyjamas. Without a word he pulled the car door open and was in the passenger's seat zipping up a windproof before I had the car in reverse.

At the corner we saw the red flashing light of the ambulance as it sped by on the road to the mine. By the time we reached the town boundary it had faded in the distance to a pulsing glow. I put my foot down and the cats' eyes began to flick past faster and faster. I held the speed at a steady hundred and twenty along the straight. After a minute or so the headlights of another car appeared in the mirror, overtaking rapidly. A mud-spattered yellow Rover surged past.

'Doctor,' said Howard out of the darkness beside me.

I nodded. The doctor's car, swaying a little, disappeared round the bend ahead. As usual he was in a great rush to get to the scene, his dignity offended because we always tried to get the ambulance officers on site first; they were much more use than he was when things went wrong underground.

Ten kilometres further on, the big white sign came into sight and I lifted my foot, changed down and swung onto the approach road to the mine. The security officer – it was Peter Kirk – had seen our lights and the boom gate was up. We shot past the gatehouse, accelerated again, then slid to a halt beside the yellow Rover outside the first-aid post.

The door was open, the long room empty, bare and antiseptic. I walked past the resuscitators, stretchers, desk and telephone, to the back door. Howard stopped at the phone to ring Kirk. I pushed the back door open, looked out. Straight ahead was the concentrator building, massive, bulky, its sparse lights darkening the bleak hills behind it. To the left lay the dim mass of workshops and stores. The other way were the muddy approaches to the main adit where it drove into the hill. A few yards away from me two men stood in a pool of light outside the door of the lamp room. They were dressed in boilersuits, hard hats and cap lamps. One of them, the doctor, was struggling irritably with his battery belt and lamp cable. Greg, the mine shift boss, was helping him. A diesel Landrover, its engine ticking over quietly, stood nearby. A few spots of rain specked its windscreen. The ambulance, of course, was long gone – through the adit and down the long spiral of the main decline.

'What happened?'

Greg looked up from the doctor's belt, shook his head.

'Rock fall,' he said. 'In the new stope off number three crosscut. Don't know how bad. But there were three men in the stope, barring down, and we've only got one out so far.'

'Shit . . .'

The doctor was standing by the Landrover, tapping his foot impatiently. He wasn't much of a doctor; he once diagnosed a groin tumour in one of the mechanics as a hernia, and tried to push it back in. But he might be of some use down below, so I jerked my head at Greg to climb into the driver's seat and the doctor scrambled in beside him. When the Landrover had disappeared I went inside the first-aid post again. Howard was just hanging up the phone.

'You better go down and have a look,' I said. Howard was the safety officer, and a very worried man. 'I'll stay here and keep an eye on things.'

He nodded and disappeared in the direction of the lamp room.

I sat down on one of the hard chairs by the desk to wait.

It was at times likes these – and they seemed to come far too often – that I wondered to myself just why I'd stayed so long on the island. I'd come here more years ago than I cared to remember, a short-term job, cleaning up the surface gossan and treating it in a simple gravity plant, just to get a cash-flow started, then I was going on to something else. But when the gossan was finished and I was ready to move on, there was nothing on offer except for the Pilbara and – God forbid – the Philippines. So I'd stayed on to get the main decline started, stayed on to commission the flotation plant, stayed on to get the crosscuts started into the big sulphide ore bodies; stayed on to marry

Gwen, to have the kids, to sink further and further into the pleasant rut of island life. Pleasant enough, except for nights like these . . .

I picked up the phone, got a line, rang the hospital to tell them that – if we were lucky – they might have a customer or two before morning. Then the police. They'd stay above ground – down there it was Mines Department territory – but the local sergeant liked to know what was going on.

Outside a light rain had set in, and the wet asphalt of the road reflected the lights in broken oily patterns. I shivered, looked at my watch. Two forty-five. I wondered what was happening down there, down that long, cold spiral of the decline, more than three hundred metres below. I wanted to go down and see, but I knew that I'd only be in the way, and that the fellows down there knew as well as I did what had to be done.

The phone on the desk rang, shrill and loud, startling me.

It was Greg, calling from the phone in the main tunnel.

'It's bad,' he said. 'The whole roof of the stope has fallen in. Rex is coming up in a few minutes, he'll talk to you. I've got to go.'

Men under the rock, he's in a hurry.

I lit a cigarette, waiting, not anxious to know the worst.

Ten minutes later a filthy Landrover pulled up outside and Rex got out, came in. He was the mine foreman, pushing sixty, half deaf from forty years of pounding drills, lungs well dusted, wise in the ways of mines and all the bad things that happen in them. His face was dirty and his spectacles were splashed with mud. He pulled off his hard hat and rubbed at the pale expanse of his exposed forehead.

'How bad?' I asked him.

'Pretty bad,' he said, squinting in the light. 'Two goners for sure. There were three of them in the stope. Two were on the tractor, one driving, one in the bucket. The other bloke was on foot, near the far wall. The driver saw it coming, bailed out, made it out through the entrance.' He paused. 'The others are still in there.'

'Any hope for them?'

'Not much. Brewster – the one who got out – saw Wilmot jump from the bucket before the rocks covered the machine. The other one . . . young Poole . . .'

The name rang a bell. 'What happened to him?'

'Brewster saw him run out from the far wall, towards the exit. He ran right under the fall. Brewster says he saw the rocks hit him.' He sighed, looking suddenly very old. 'You tell them and you tell them . . .'

I knew what he meant. We tried to drum it into everyone who went down the hole – if there's a fall, stay close to the walls. But they never do . . .

'No hope at all?' I said.

'No,' said Rex, 'there's three or four metres of rock on top of him.'

'You started digging?'

'Yep. But we've got to be careful in case there's another fall. I'd better get back.'

He got as far as the door before I stopped him.

'How long has Tony Poole been barring down?'

Rex looked a little uncomfortable. 'Quite a while . . .'

'Three months? More?'

He said nothing for a moment. Then: 'You'd better talk to Alan Kent.'

I thought about that for a moment or two. 'Alan kept him on it? All this time?'

He nodded.

'Rex,' I said, 'I'm going to have to call the Mines Inspector. He'll probably fly in in the morning. He's going to give you a hard time.'

He shrugged, turned away, went out.

I rang the gatehouse, and Kirk told me that he'd phoned Kent soon after calling me. He couldn't be far away now. And he had some questions to answer.

Barring down.

Except for raise-climbing, it's the worst, dirtiest, most dangerous job in the mine. The raise-climbers are the aristocrats of the contract miners, and paid accordingly. But barring down, well, it's the first job you get, usually, after you've driven a service tractor for a month or two. And generally you get moved on after you've done a month or so.

What happens is that a small gang, usually three men, goes into a stope straight after it's been drilled, blasted and cleared. One drives the loader, another stands in the bucket with a crowbar, and the third acts as the clean-up man. The driver raises the bucket till his mate can reach the roof. He in turn uses his bar to prise away the loose bits of the roof that have been left hanging. In good ground it's no problem. But when the ground is bad, half the roof can come down on you with almost no warning.

Not a job you'd want to stay on longer than you have to.

I heard the car approaching, revving high as it came down through the gears, coming to a halt in a swirl of gravel just outside the first-aid post. A door slammed, footsteps on the walkway, and there he was, God's gift to the island.

Twenty-eight years old, tall and blond, good-looking except for the eyes – too small and set too close together. Three o'clock on a wet and dismal morning and he was dressed as if he was going to the Squatters' Ball. He flicked rain from his lapels, sat on the edge of a table.

'What's the score?'

Could have been a cricket match from the tone of his voice.

I didn't like him. He'd been given the job because his family owned ten per cent of the company's shares, had held them from the old days when the mine was nothing but a tiny scratch on the landscape. After graduating he'd gone to Mount Isa, then, when this job had fallen vacant, he'd come back to the island.

I'd talked to someone I knew at Mount Isa, and got a commiserating laugh. Total prick, that was the judgment, and in the twelve months he'd been with us as Mine Engineer, nothing had happened that would have changed their minds.

He knew what tonight's score was, alright – he would have stopped at the gatehouse on his way in.

'One out,' I said. 'Two still down there under the rock. Percy Wilmot, and your mate Tony Poole.'

'Not my mate,' he said, not meeting my eye.

'No,' I said. 'I didn't think so. Not the way you kept him barring down for six months or so.'

He didn't say anything.

'And not the way he took your girl,' I said.

He flushed then, and turned away. 'He didn't take her,' he said. 'And anyway, she wasn't my girl.'

'Well,' I said, 'she's nobody's girl now.'

He stood staring out the window, saying nothing.

'You did a real bloody Uriah on him, didn't you?'

'A what?'

'Never read your Bible, I suppose, did you? Second Samuel? King David, sniffing like a randy dog round Uriah's wife? "Set him in the forefront of the hottest battle, and retire ye from him, that he may be smitten . . ."'

He looked blank, as if it was all a foreign language to him.

'You really are a prick, aren't you?' I said.

Kay was a teacher, not too long out of college. Straight fair hair cut off below the ears. A straight back, no-nonsense blue eyes. Not pretty, not beautiful, something better than that, a kind of deep, trans- parent honesty that gave her a kind of shine.

Kent had fastened onto her like a limpet; took her to all the parties, all the barbecues, all the dances. Took her fishing in his fancy boat, driving in his Jag, flying in his little Cessna. A well-matched pair, until you looked closely.

Tony Poole ended all that. I heard she met him after the first football match of the season. Saw him play. Oh, he was a lovely footballer, Tony. She went up to him at the barbecue afterwards, talked to him for a while. And that was that. All the drives then were in Tony's old ute, all the fishing from his old man's tinny. They looked so bloody happy together . . .

Of course, it was a great blow to Kent's pride. His girl pinched by an Abo miner.

You couldn't say, of course, that Kent had killed the boy. Nothing as strong as that. But when we had cave- ins, they were nearly always in new stopes. And if you were barring down, then you spent a lot of time in new stopes. I thought then, and I think now, that Kent was too gutless a creature actually to plan to kill any- one at all, even Poole. It was mostly just plain bloody- minded meanness on his part, keeping someone he didn't like – especially an Aborigine – in an unpleasant job as long as possible, maybe even force him to toss in his job.

And I might have said more to him then, but the phone rang.

It was Rex, very excited. 'We've got one out – he's alive!'

'Who?' In a way, I didn't want to know, because to know was somehow to condemn the other one to death.

'Wilmot,' said Rex. 'He was in the bucket, jumped and rolled under the tractor. We've just dug him out. Shaken up, but not a bone broken.'

'And Poole?'

Silence.

They brought Wilmot up to the surface a quarter of an hour later, wrapped in a blanket. The doctor was with him, fussing; he'd got someone to play with at last. Wilmot, a short, thickset fellow in his thirties, had the shakes. But he was grinning his head off. Just sat in the chair, grinning and grinning, shaking and shaking. 'That's it,' he kept on saying, 'that's it, I'm never going back down there . . .'

They packed him off in the ambulance.

The doctor came in, tramping mud all over the clean linoleum. Everyone else did that too, but with the doctor it irritated me.

'I'm going home,' he said. 'Call me when you dig the other one out.' He stumped off, and a few moments later the yellow Rover roared off into the night.

Kent was still standing by the window, looking out into the night. Or, more likely, staring at his own reflection. I wondered briefly just what he was thinking about. Perhaps Poole, perhaps the girl. More likely about himself. The truth was, he had more in common with Poole than just the girl. Not that he would ever admit it to himself, or anyone else. Everyone on the island had secrets. Gwen found out all about that when she started researching the old island records . . .

The lights of a Landrover played over the wet gravel of the yard, as it left the main adit. It pulled up outside and Howard came in, muddy and wet. I could imagine what it was like down there now. They were through the country rock and into the ore body, and in the new stope the harsh light of the emergency lamps would be playing on the shining walls of freshly cleaved ore. There was a lot of arsenopyrite in that lode, which gave the ore a shining, silvery look, and there would be that faint rotten-egg smell of arsenic. There would be as many men as could work in the confined space, levering the great chunks aside, throwing the small ones back into the loader bucket. They'd be working mostly in silence, and with a serious intensity, breathing hard, sweating heavily, hoping for a miracle, yet knowing all the time that this morning all the miracles had been used up.

I've never liked working underground, although I've done it all my adult life. And the sky, night or day, wet or dry, is always a kind of blessing when you come to the surface again.

'How did it happen?' I asked Howard. Kent turned to face us.

Howard shook his head. 'God knows. There was no warning, and Rex checked the stope at the beginning of the shift. Maybe an earth movement, a subsidence . . . Have you called the Mines Department?'

I nodded. 'They'll have an inspector on the morning plane.'

Someone called to Howard from outside, and he pulled back his shoulders, drew himself up a little straighter, turned and went out.

'What now?' It was Kent, from his place by the window.

'This is your first one, isn't it? Never seen one before?'

He shook his head.

'Put your overalls on,' I said. 'Get a ride down to the stope. Stay there. Don't try to help, you'll only get in the way. Just stay there and watch.'

'How long?'

'Till they dig him out,' I said. 'I want you to see him when they dig him out.'

'I'll just get a cup of coffee . . .'

'No,' I said, 'you'll get into your fucking overalls and get down there *now*.'

For a moment I thought he was going to argue. But he didn't.

When he was gone I sat down, lit a cigarette, and thought about the phone call I would have to make. Poole's father, Eric, would have to be told, and soon. Wonderful part of my job, that sort of thing, ringing people up before dawn, telling them their son's been crushed to death in a rockfall. Waiting wasn't going to make it any better, so I picked up the phone book, looked up the number, dialled.

It rang for a long time before Eric answered.

After I told him what had happened he was silent for a bit.

'Any hope, Barney?' he said at last. 'Any hope at all?'

'No,' I said. 'I'm sorry.'

There was another long silence.

'What happens now?' he said.

'We're working hard to recover his body. As soon as we do, I'll call you.'

'What about Kay? Are you going to call her?'

She was living with another girl at the hostel behind the school. 'If you like,' I said. 'I thought I'd get my wife to go round to see her, later on.'

'It's alright,' he said. 'The wife and I will do it. But not yet. Best let her sleep as long as she can.'

'I'm more sorry than I can say, Eric. I liked him, we all liked him . . .'

But he had already put the phone down.

Tony was the only son, the only child.

When I looked out the window, there was the first hint of light, false dawn, in the sky beyond the crusher. The clouds were gone, the wind had dropped, and it was going to be a fine day. A fine day, but a bloody miserable one.

Eric Poole had worked for the Ag Bank for more than twenty years, and everyone said he was the best foreman they'd ever had. Even if he was an Aborigine. There was always that qualification on the island. Well, there's always been a job at the mine for any of the local blacks, I've seen to that. But not many of them stay for long. Sooner or later work seems to conflict with other urgencies they have – the birding season, or more money on the boats, or just restlessness. Tony Poole was different; you could see that he would be as good and as steady as his dad. Started as a trades assistant before he moved to the mining side. Never missed a day's work in nearly a year. Not until he turned twenty-one and they had a birthday party for him. It went on all weekend, and he missed work on the Monday.

So Kent sacked him.

I only found out about it when Eric Poole rang me, told me what had happened. 'Tell him to turn up tomorrow,' I said. 'Just pretend nothing happened. He'll lose a day's pay, that's all.'

I put the phone down, walked down the corridor to Kent's office. He was sitting there, looking at assay reports from the new lode.

'Why did you sack Tony Poole?' I asked.

He glanced up, shrugged. 'He had a skinful last weekend, missed work. No room for a drunk down the mine.'

'When are you going to sack Wally Nason?' I said. 'Or Nugget Wilkes? Lucky to see either of them any Monday of the year. So why just Poole?'

He said nothing.

'He'll be back on the job tomorrow,' I said. 'Fix it up with the paymaster. And if you ever try anything like that again, you'll be out the gate yourself.'

He flushed, and his lips set in a thin line.

The next day Tony Poole was back on the job. Barring down. And still there nearly six months later.

Full light, now, and I looked at my watch. Almost seven, time to start making more phone calls. Almost. Another cup of coffee first. The mine wouldn't work today. The town would be quiet, the pubs crowded, but the crowds subdued. Gwen would be round early to see the Pooles. Not just a duty. She's like that, cares about people.

Sometimes I think that I should have gone to the Pilbara years ago. Or some other open cut, where you never have to go underground and everything happens out in the open.

Those old island families, like the Kents. It was Gwen, of course, a long time ago, years and years, who let me into the big secret. Our kids away at school every day, she was a bit bored, needing something new to occupy her time. Started researching her own family – she's not old island, her father was a soldier settler from western New South Wales – then turned to the island's history, dug into the council records, church records, registrar's records. And when that wasn't enough, didn't go far enough back, she went to the mainland, to the State archives.

It was three days before she came back, and when she got off the plane I noticed that she was a little subdued. That night, when the kids were in bed and the house was quiet I poured her a glass of wine and put it on the coffee table beside her.

'You'd better tell me,' I said. 'What is it?'

She picked up the glass, sipped at the wine, put it down again.

'I'm going to burn my notes,' she said. 'It was a bad idea. I'm just going to forget the whole thing.'

'Nearly three months' work down the drain?'

She shrugged.

'What did you find out?'

She took another drink of wine. 'I should have guessed,' she said, 'when I couldn't find any of the early records – the really early ones – on the island.'

'Should have guessed what?'

'Nearly all the old island families, the ones that have been here since the early eighteen-hundreds, they've nearly all got a bit of Aboriginal blood. Way back, and just a little, but it's there.'

I shouldn't have been surprised, I suppose. The first white men here were sealers, and they brought their Aboriginal women from the mainland. We sat there in silence for a while.

'I think you're right,' I said at last. 'Best to burn the notes.'

I never asked for any of the details. Not till years later, when Kay left Alan Kent for Tony Poole. I asked Gwen then, about Alan Kent.

She looked at me for a long moment before she spoke.

'He's got a black great-great-grandmother,' she said.

It explained a lot of things, of course. Not just about Kent, but about all the old families. They hate the blacks even more than the soldier settlers ever did, and most of *them* came from Walgett and points west. Those old families . . . the Kents, the Sorells, the Bricknells and Pertwees, the Mayfields and the Leakes, the island's aristocracy – that's how they saw themselves – it must have been festering in them for generations, far below the surface, never acknowledged, never admitted. Probably didn't know, some of them, not for sure, just that horrible suspicion that if they looked far enough back, they might find something so unpleasant that it would destroy their own vision of themselves.

Rex phoned me at a little after ten o'clock. They were getting close, and he knew I would want to be there.

There was no traffic in the decline, and it was quiet except for the sound of the Landrover's engine booming back off the rock walls. I parked behind the other vehicles and walked down to the crosscut.

The men had stopped work and were standing round in silent groups. The floor of the stope was almost cleared, only a low pile of rock left in the centre. Howard was standing here with Rex, a stretcher at their feet. I walked past Kent and stopped beside Howard.

'We waited for you,' he said.

'Thanks.' For nothing.

Rex beckoned to the nearest group of miners. Their navy boilersuits were soaked and stained, their dirt-streaked faces gaunt and tired. They started to clear away the last of the rocks. When the body appeared I looked round for Kent. He had turned away, moved towards the exit. I went after him, dragged him back, stood him next to the body. He began to vomit when they put it on the stretcher, and I let him go then.

Up on the surface again I stood for a few moments, taking deep breaths, sucking in the cold morning air as if I couldn't get enough of it. I felt like heading off to the pub, where most of the others would be going. But the company pays me a good salary, and it was one of those days when I would earn every cent of it.

On the day of the funeral the wind stormed in from the west, and when we got out of the car at the gates of the cemetery on Vinegar Hill the horizon was lost in a swirl of rainclouds. The rain began before the service did, sweeping in from the sea. Kay was standing by the graveside with Eric Poole and his wife. Her face was wet, but I couldn't tell if it was tears or rain. She was holding Dulcie Poole's arm, and I could tell that Dulcie was on the point of collapse. She was a good, strong girl, Kay, and faced the grave and the rain and the stares with her head up and her back straight.

Alan Kent wasn't there, and I was glad of it.

A week later the inquest was held. Kent had to be there then, to answer the coroner's questions. The coroner, who was also the local health inspector, ran the slowest inquests I've ever seen. His girlfriend, the baker's wife, sat behind a typewriter and typed everything that was said. You had to speak very slowly and clearly, and you had to repeat yourself a lot. It made for a long day.

The coroner found for accidental death, commiserated with the family, praised the company's safety procedures, and waffled for five minutes about the dangers implicit in working half a kilometre below ground. As if we didn't know.

After it was over I found Alan Kent standing on the footpath outside the courthouse. The rain had stopped the day before and now the sun shone reluctantly. I went up and stood beside him.

'You're finished here,' I said. 'I don't even want you on the site again. I'll get someone to clean out your desk.'

'You can't do that,' he said. And he seemed to believe it. They're an arrogant lot, the old families.

'I just did,' I said.

'My father, he'll call the chairman . . .'

'Your father,' I said, 'can save himself the trouble. The chairman would rather lose you than me.'

I left him standing on the footpath with his mouth open. He flew off to the mainland the next morning, and I haven't seen him since. Kay was on the same plane, but according to the other passengers she never spoke to him, never even looked at him the whole flight.

The Whippet and the Willow

Gillian **Mears**

Emily Egan lies underneath the rug made out of the six hundred and thirty-six hexagons she crocheted when the whippet was no more than a puppy. He is an old dog now and the rug smells of his skin and her skin, or of an intermingling of the two, one indistinguishable from the other, but not at all unpleasant. When Emily strokes her whippet's head she often thinks of Eileen, who gave the dog to her almost sixteen years ago, and whose skin had had a similar silkiness. One of the qualities that had drawn Eileen to a whippet in the first place was that it didn't have the strong odour of most other breeds.

Emily Egan's hand moves from his head to her own arm where she can feel the tiny tumours spreading. They remind her of a skin rash Cappy once developed after racing through a patch of stinging nettles. The vet bill had taken most of her pension and that week they'd lived on baby grunters caught from the Mary Street wharf. Although the doctor has told her that the lumps are nothing to fear, Emily can't help equating them with the ones her father once made her feel years ago under the tail of the old grey gelding who had to be shot.

A whippet which looks so frail on the ground is far from small and inconspicuous in bed. It feels like the dog is growing bigger every night as he groans with pleasure at being so warm and stretches out his legs. Once, quite recently, Cappy pushed her out of the bed and she landed on the floor of the caravan like a baby bird out of its nest. It's difficult to sleep tonight because there has been a complaint. Someone has written a letter to Mr Johns about the presence of a dog in the Poplar Tree Caravan Park. There have been complaints before, of course, but never of a formal kind. That someone has gone to the bother of a letter and an envelope perturbs Emily as much as that she doesn't know who the person is. She lies with her eyes shut, thinking of a figure hunched over a letter, his face darkened by a dislike of dogs.

At nine o'clock Emily hears the night time ice-cream van going past the gates of the caravan park. 'Too cold for ice-cream, eh Cappy,' she says and half rising, opens the door of the small fridge that is next to the bed. She offers the whippet some leftover vermicelli and sweetened milk pudding. It is still lukewarm. 'Nice isn't it, darling. Go on, you finish it. I had plenty.' The dog's teeth clink on the teaspoon in a way that Emily Egan finds more comforting than the slightly mournful note of the ice-cream truck bells.

Mr Johns said that complaints always came from those you'd least expect. Mr Johns, who had a soft spot for Cappy because he'd once had racing whippets, said that what they might have to do is put a little fence up around the van so that Cappy didn't go wandering, possibly lifting his leg on Mr Marsden's marigolds.

'So it was Mr Marsden!' Emily had said. 'And I always thought he was such a kind gentleman.'

'No. Oh no,' Mr Johns had replied, in a tone of voice that indicated Mr Marsden would be the least likely resident of the whole of Poplar Tree Caravan Park to put in a complaint.

Although Emily had begged Mr Johns to tell her who the complainant was, he'd said that she wasn't to worry, the information was Private and Confidential. He said he would go to see the person and talk rationally, pointing out that Emily and Cappy were the Poplar Tree Caravan Park's most loved senior citizens. Only in the event of a further letter would Mr Johns think about fencing in Emily Egan's whippet. 'And we wouldn't like that to have to happen to our Mr Cap, would we now?' he'd said, smoothing his hand on Cappy all the way from his face to his tail so that the whippet had half collapsed against his leg with pleasure.

Emily Egan's caravan is the ancient green one tucked in under the willow tree near the water. It is the kind of quaint, curved timber structure that makes people driving past – who generally look down their noses at caravans or their dwellers – imagine putting a van of that shape at the bottom of the garden. They think about it in terms of an extra room for the child who has recently become impossible. The wife will crane her neck to keep Emily Egan's caravan in view, thinking that it would be a delightfully small area to renovate and decorate and to hang with curtains appropriate for a fifteen-year-old son. Something with soldiers or trumpets, she thinks, as she gets one last glimpse of the van and her husband demands to know what has taken her interest.

It's as if the curved shape of the willow tree has taken its shape from Emily Egan's home. This effect is heightened now that it's autumn and the tree is losing its leaves. Once an artist travelling north from Sydney stopped to paint the river and painted Emily Egan's van instead, using strangely thick gouache and selling it for one thousand dollars at his opening night.

Lines of black ants wend their way all night from the willow's trunk and across the green plywood, before disappearing through the small oval that Emily Egan calls the kitchen window. At one time she'd found a sticker of a carrot, a radish and an onion in the bottom of a discarded showbag and had put that over the glass. These peeled off a long time ago and as the ants pass over the glass, their legs are only momentarily slowed down by traces of old glue.

From the three-quarter size bed, Emily can see the half full moon. The way it's positioned behind the willow gives the painful impression that the moon is being stretched longer by the tree's limbs. At some point in the night she knows some of the ants will begin to die; or rather, she thinks, the ants who come so steadily into her van are the actual carriers of the dead. Whether it is that the ants die or are transported, every night they fall from the ceiling onto her bed. They are like a pale tidemark she must shake out from her bed every morning, for after death, their colour fades from black to brown. This fading makes Emily think of the way a tattoo grows faint on an old person's skin.

When a flea bites her under the arm she tells the whippet that it is a shower day for him tomorrow. She thinks with affection of Mr Johns, who turns a blind eye to Emily taking her shower with Cappy. This is by far the easiest method of washing a whippet. Emily Egan holds him lightly between her legs and shifts sideways to allow warm water to stream onto the dog. She tips his face and his ears away and begins to froth him up with her own shampoo which is pink and smells of roses. After his shower he behaves like he's less than a year old. He sprints around a few caravans and back to Emily Egan like the champion he would've been, says Mr Johns, if he'd ever raced.

With the flea held between her fingers, Emily gets out of bed to drown it in a cup of water. Soon it will be too cold for them. She looks over to the Young Girl's on-site van. The Young Girl has hung the windows with tea towels that only cover the glass three-quarters of the way. Emily can see her at night, writing madly. She's sure it couldn't have been the Young Girl who put in the complaint, since the Young Girl's son loves Cappy so much. Only yesterday, the little boy was delighted. 'Look at Cappy,' he said, 'getting up in his pretty dressing gown.' For Emily Egan had put on his autumn coat, crocheted in red, in river stitch, and tied up with a green bow. It seems to Emily as if the Young Girl's child understands the fragility of whippets, their soft sense of humour. She has seen him trying to catch the shadow of Cappy's long tail in the afternoons on the beach.

No, worries Emily, it couldn't be the Young Girl. And nor, she is sure, could it have been the German women, travelling around Australia on gold and purple mountain bikes. She can't believe it would be one of them, not even if they'd ridden over one of Cappy's small droppings. For a moment Emily Egan even contemplates putting her dress back on and going over to their purple tent and checking with them but the whippet groans from the bed, as if to say, oh Emily, don't fret. She can't think of who else it might be. She has lost track of all the residents. There are so many relocatable cabins coming and old vans moving to the caravan park not on the river, where the weekly rate isn't so expensive.

One thing living in the Poplar Tree Caravan Park has taught Emily Egan is that life is unfair. She squeezes herself back into bed next to her dog and thinks for instance about the kind of woman who, upon entering a toilet cubicle of the Ladies, immediately begins to sigh loudly over an unclean seat. Yet it is exactly that kind of woman who, in the process of hovering rather than sitting on the seat, messes it up for everyone else. Sometimes, when Emily's bad eyesight has led her to sitting unsuspecting upon a splashed seat, she wishes that next to the graffiti about sex she could add her own. Who are the Peeing Hypocrites? she imagines writing in thick red crayon, and thinks Eileen would've enjoyed that question.

In the morning a deep mist covers the river. Emily Egan laughs to see her dog. His ears look bigger in the early mornings, as if like a child his hair has been pulled back in the night from his ears to reveal their full size. There are drowned ants and the smell of electricity in the old kookaburra jug. 'Oh dear,' says Emily. 'You poor things.' She finds a single strand spiderweb has been built across the rim of her teacup. She drinks from the other side of the cup and watches the web. It dips in and out, re-emerging with small tea drops like flashes of dew. On mornings such as this one, when the far river bank is invisible, Emily Egan thinks that she is travelling on water, in a round green boat far away from the gates of the Poplar Tree Caravan Park. Her caravan would have a simple white sail or a small putting motor and at the front, Cappy, as elegant a figurehead as any boat could want. She imagines sailing up river where they would settle far from the complaints of the world. For want of any better name, she calls this place The Abandoned Garden. So far up the river there would be no red and white speedboats with people talking in loud and boastful voices. In The Abandoned Garden small whirly-whirlies of grass would send Cappy into the same excited twists. Emily Egan wouldn't even worry about a toilet but would squat outside and feel the tickly blades of grass on her bottom.

Mrs Tathra sits on a stool behind white lace curtains, talking on the phone to her mother. She owns the largest relocatable home in the park with a red roof and yellow walls. The crackle of sugar in her mother's mouth annoys her almost as much as the appearance of Emily Egan, coming outside with breakfast for the dog. 'She's feeding it out of one of her own bowls,' Mrs Tathra tells her mother. 'I wish you wouldn't eat sugar when I'm on the phone.'

'What about the complaint you put in?'

'Says he'll do something but he's as dotty about the dog as she is. Told me to think about an old lady's feelings. So I wrote another letter last night. Oh, seeing it was doing its business all around the palms, that was the last straw.'

'I don't know why she's allowed a dog,' which is what her mother always says when Mrs Tathra whinges about Emily Egan. 'There's that big sign up on the gates saying no animals. Only caged birds, isn't that right?'

Mrs Tathra can hear her mother sucking at the sugar and the sound is nearly driving her crazy.

'And how's Baxter?' asks her mother. 'Tell him he hasn't been to see me for months. Anyone'd think I lived ten hours not ten minutes away.'

But Mrs Tathra won't be distracted from Emily Egan who is bending over Cappy, unsnapping the nappy pin which fastens the coat at the front. The nappy pin is bent beyond use yet somehow, each morning and evening, Emily Egan – who turns eighty next month – wrestles it open and shut. 'Do you remember,' says Mrs Tathra, 'that whippet that tried to bite me at the bus-stop? It used to wear a little coat too. Purple and green stripes.'

'What's Baxter up to today? Has he got a word for his Nan?'

When Mrs Tathra turns around to look at her son she feels he's looking right through the loose shirt she wears over her pink gym shorts. He sits at the table, shovelling Choc Dot Crispies into his mouth. She waves the phone receiver at him but now she's facing him directly, he eats as if she doesn't exist.

'No doubt he'll be going fishing again. All he seems interested in at the moment. He is annoying,' says Mrs Tathra without specifying the windchimes or anything else. She moves with the telephone to the dresser decorated with hockey trophies and xeroxed copies of Baxter's ancestors who she has lovingly put inside gold trim photo frames. One of them has a moustache in the shape of Baxter's but on the whole Baxter is altogether of a much weedier build and even his hair lacks the thick lustre of his great-grandfather.

Mrs Tathra doesn't know why her son ties up the windchimes which he made at his last year at school for Mother's Day. Or why his jeans are full of gravel that finds its way into the carpet, the washing machine and even the bowl of the toilet, so that for a while Mrs Tathra thought she'd been passing stones. She has never asked her son for the answers to these questions.

The conversation with her mother begins to wind up with the usual talk about housekeeping. Mrs Tathra tells how she would love to get into Emily Egan's caravan when she and the dog weren't there and scrub it down with Ajax and boiling water. 'It might be more bearable then,' she says, though she has never been inside Emily Egan's van. If Mrs Tathra takes meat scraps down to Emily Egan's, Emily Egan always stands squarely in front of the door. Although her voice is soft and she is frail, the woollen clothes she wears mean that Mrs Tathra can't for the life of her ever get a peep inside.

'This caravan park isn't a gravy kitchen for dogs,' Mrs Tathra had written last night to Mr Johns and thought her note of sarcasm in the letter was rather clever. She had written that, even though she's often thought it convenient having the whippet in the park for meat scraps. It stops her garbage bin gathering smells. Less definable to Mrs Tathra is the memory of last time she took scraps down for the whippet. Emily had urged Mrs Tathra to feed the rinds to Cappy herself and there was something rather pleasant, Mrs Tathra had to admit, about the way its delicate pink tongue licked the grease off her fingers.

'Listen,' says Mrs Tathra's mother, 'what could I get Baxter for his birthday? What about some shaving soap?'

'I wouldn't have a clue, Mum. I think he might even be growing a beard looking at him this morning.'

Mrs Tathra wouldn't have a clue about most of Baxter's wishes. The way he has taken to bursting into the bathroom to stare with scorn at Mrs Tathra's small breast is something she doesn't like to think about. Once he'd even crossed the bathmat and roughly squeezed the breast. He'd been on as a casual at the mill at the time and she'd felt the torn callouses of his hand meet her soft skin. When her nipple hardened the look on his face was half pleased, half repulsed. In a fluster she'd pulled her towel tight around her body and searched in the bathroom cabinet for something for his hands. By the time she'd found an old bottle of liniment he was revving up his car and squealing off in a way she feared would lead to complaints against her own tidy home. She hadn't even heard Baxter leave the bathroom. He could be like that. Noisy one moment; creeping the next. She doesn't like to remember how on that night she'd taken off all her nightclothes, thinking that when he got home he might again come into her bed as if he was a small child again, of how it wouldn't be as a small child that he'd come.

'Look at that bloody whippet would you,' says Mrs Tathra, taking the cereal bowl away from Baxter. 'Now she's put its coat back on again. Doesn't know if she's Arthur or Martha this morning. Would you like some eggs?' Through the leftover chocolate-flavoured milk she sees the extra sugar he has added like a drift of white sand. 'You're just like your nan. Love sugar. I can't understand how your teeth put up with it. She'd love it if you popped over today. Wants to know what to get you for your birthday.'

But her son only looks indifferently at her and resumes picking at his face in the cosmetics mirror he has taken from her bedroom.

This morning it's as if Emily Egan occasionally senses the vehemence of Mrs Tathra's gaze. Cappy too becomes uneasy, tucking his tail in tight between his back legs and not licking clean his gravy. 'Come on darling,' pleads Emily. 'You're nothing but skin and bones.' The dog lifts one foot and like a horse, paws the ground lightly. This is the cue for Emily Egan to throw a soft toy for the whippet to fetch. She watches with pleasure the way he bounds away, his coat such a bright dash of colour against the bare patch in the lawn he is like an autumn leaf.

Mrs Tathra has seen toys lying about the grass around Emily Egan's van that are thick with dried dog spit and grass. In a way she thinks it is like having an untidy family living in the middle of the view. Some of the soft toys are left to lie so long that grass grows violently through their bellies. 'Where are you off to today, Bax?' she asks.

Grunting an indecipherable reply, Baxter grabs the lunchbox she has made up for him the night before and slams out of the house without taking the bag of food scraps for the dog. With relief, Mrs Tathra turns on her aerobics video. There will come a time, she feels sure, when her son won't talk to her at all and they will live together in such a total silence Mrs Tathra feels scared. It would be nice, she thinks, if he does catch a little shark today. That's what he's been fishing for, she knows, because the butcher has mentioned how Baxter's been in buying blood and guts for berley.

A bit of fresh flake in her beer batter might put him in better spirits. Chips just this side of burnt, the way he's always preferred. The smell of burning oil in her home would be worth it if it would bring back her smiling Baxter boy.

She listens to the young American voice of the instructor psyching her into an energetic state. Beyond Emily Egan's van a waterskier has begun to warm into some fancy tricks on the river. Waterskiers have good legs. In Baxter's bedroom the home gym she gave him for Christmas would be thick with dust but for the fact she gives his room a thorough clean every Friday night when she can be sure he won't be home until the early hours of Saturday morning. When she moves her gaze back to Emily Egan, she sees the old woman disappearing into the Ladies. At this moment she

notices that her son is still in the caravan park, waiting it seems for something or somebody, as he lets his
car idle. Then he's getting out of his car and bending
towards the whippet, making, of all things, motions of
friendliness.

'Well, why wouldn't he . . .' begins Mrs Tathra
helplessly, thinking of the meat scraps. Mrs Tathra
sees her son clicking his fingers. On automatic, she
begins to warm up to the music, energetically lifting
her knees to hit her hands which she keeps at hip
height. Her son looks a bit like a rodent himself, she
sees. All he'd need would be a rat's tail like the dog.

Baxter bundles the dog into the back of his car with
such roughness she fears one of the dog's stick-like
legs will break. As she watches, she feels a mixture of
emotions. For once, she convinces herself, in order to
feel a brief surge of pleasure, Baxter is thinking of me.
Then this feeling quickly fades as she wonders would
she act any differently if she'd been watching her son
push a girl into his car so roughly. By the time Emily
Egan emerges, her son and the dog have gone. The
caravan park seems to settle down easily to their
absence. Everything about the view looks totally
normal.

Emily presses the bones of her bottom up into the old
red bricks. One of the German girls is having a
shower. Emily can hear the girl's wonderful voice,
singing something in her own language with a bit of
English thrown in every now and again. The wool of

the crocheted dress is getting too hot in the sun. She crouches, waiting for her dog. Sometimes Cappy hits her so hard when he does appear, the bones in her back make a loud cracking sound. Then for the rest of the morning she'll call him The Chiropractor.

'Cappy,' Emily calls. It doesn't usually take him so long. She peers around and watches a waterskier being towed. She used to hate their racket but now her eyes are going, she sees them as rather plaintive shapes, their arms stretched out as if to beg for something that only the roaring engines might be able to give. Emily Egan looks up to Mrs Tathra's, wondering if her friend's got any meat for Cappy today.

Mrs Tathra sits at the table. The cloth is spattered with cereal and milk, as if a child of ten, not a thirty-year-old man, had been eating here. She picks up the hand mirror. Three popped blackheads haven't been wiped off its surface. It is too revolting. She finds a handkerchief and then looks critically at the dark bristles regrowing on her chin. As she glances out the window, she can't locate Emily Egan. Baxter is only playing some kind of a prank. The dog will be back in no time at all. In the mirror she sees the way the lines above her top lip run vertically and deep and that these lines are repeated at either side of her chin. She seizes the bristle with the most growth and yanks it out. The next five minutes are spent in futile pursuit of the other hairs that, rather than succumb to the tweezer's will, get pushed back into the follicle. It is enough to make a woman scream. Mrs Tathra raises the mirror to look at where the rinse from the chemist has turned her grey temples a kind of dead mulberry colour rather than the promised vibrant deep brown.

'I could clean the bathroom,' suggests Mrs Tathra to the empty room. But the glimpse she catches of Emily Egan setting off down the road is too distracting. The old lady is heading for town, whereas Mrs Tathra knows her son would've been going to the wharf on the edge of town, where he does all his fishing.

The Flick man would be the ideal solution for Emily Egan's entire van, thinks Mrs Tathra. Just one flick. Once, when she was a fully breasted woman, still married to Mr Tathra, she'd had a Naughty with a Flick man. After he'd sprayed for redbacks in Mr Tathra's rockery, she'd bowed to the pressure of the Flick man's fingers squeezing into her arm. It has even occurred to Mrs Tathra that it was the spider poison and that episode's stress that led to her cancer. Every time she drives past the billboard on the northern approach to town, which pictures a frightened cockroach, she remembers how the Flick man's neck had smelt of poison and of how long he'd taken getting it over and done with as Mrs Tathra's eyes scanned the open front door and she prayed no visitor would pop over.

Mrs Tathra takes the letter to Mr Johns out of the envelope. She finds three spelling mistakes. To the disco beat of the video she briskly types the whole thing out again. Baxter might've taken the dog away for the morning but by tonight the joke will be over and the same problems will exist. She has listed these in point form so that this time Mr Johns might take her a little more seriously. She has also collected signatures for a petition but wonders about the worth of including this since only the Munns and Whittakers, problem residents in their own right, would sign.

Mrs Tathra makes her way cautiously down the hill to Emily Egan's caravan under the willow tree. In her shirt pocket is the freshly addressed envelope and in her hand she carries some of last night's leftover chicken. Should Emily Egan return to her van without Mrs Tathra's knowledge, she can then hold up the scraps and say she'd thought the dog might want them.

The faint smell of dog hair and wool that greets Mrs Tathra's nose when she stands at the door is mild and almost pleasing. But it is shocking, she reminds herself – an old woman and an old dog. The bed is a rumpled mess of crocheting in progress and rugs already so old their squares are pulling away from their partners. Or it's as if the violent clash of colours is flinging them apart. Mrs Tathra's finger goes up to her chin. The damned bristle has popped out again. She looks in vain around Emily Egan's van for a mirror. She can see a mark on the wall that is mirror-shaped but the mirror itself is nowhere in sight. All she can find is a shiny spot in the teapot but in this, her face warps and recedes from her in a way she finds so disturbing she sits down for a moment on the edge of the bed. The small fridge which she pulls open is empty except for some kind of food, laid out in a line along the middle racks. Using the tips of her nails she picks up one and then another. They are old crackers with a piece of smoked oyster stuck on each. Hepatitis A, thinks Mrs Tathra, and she wonders could the Health Department be brought around. Under the bed, she is sure Cappy's dog bowl is Emily Egan's chamber pot.

Now that she has begun to snoop she finds that she can't stop. The cupboards at shoulder height above the bed are too enticing. There is a feeling of opening a doll's house, they are so tiny.

Here are some photos. Mrs Tathra doesn't treat the old album daintily but rather flicks through it so that some of the photographs fall out of their corners. She can hear her own breathing gather pace. She sees Emily Egan at some kind of dog fair, where the whippet, dressed in a wedding dress, has won the competition. She sees a photo which unmistakably shows Emily Egan, at an age too old for kissing, passionately doing so to a woman with white hair tied back into a ponytail. She'd always wondered why there was never any mention of a Mr Egan. At the back of the album is a loose enlargement of the dog in its gown. How sick, thinks Mrs Tathra, for the whippet is a boy dog, even if some long ago vet did cut out its balls and tuck the remaining skin into the shape of a neat grey purse. In the background of the photo, though less in focus, Mrs Tathra can see other weirdos with other dogs dressed up as various things.

'The old lezzo.' The words come whistling out of Mrs Tathra.

Emily Egan runs. It is hot in her dress and she doesn't know in what direction the danger to Cappy lies. She can feel the sweat beginning to saturate her under-clothes. There is a drift of cloud this morning, she notices, as grey and soft as Cappy's muzzle. She wishes that she was looking for her dog in The Abandoned Garden. If I was looking for him there, she thinks, I'd tear off this woollen dress and run more swiftly. She imagines that she is there and that she is a child, running barefoot on a pebble road. She is so light the pebbles don't affect the skin of her feet.

Outside the corner shop where she stops there are real children, all unwrapping ice-creams.

'Have any of you seen a little greyhound type of a dog?' Emily Egan makes wild motions with her hands. Into her mind comes springing an image of Cappy as a puppy in her arms, always being mistaken for some kind of kangaroo. 'Looks a bit like a wallaby. Have you seen a little dog like that? White markings on his head and chest?'

The children shake their heads and eat their icypoles which are in the shape of giant pencils. She listens to their feet shifting this way and that on the cement and suddenly feels sure they are counting down the seconds between life and death.

Other images of Cappy arrive in Emily Egan's mind as she abruptly leaves the children and changes the direction of her search. She thinks it's as if she has become Cappy, and that as she is about to die, her past life is flowing like bright water through her mind. She remembers the day Eileen gave her the puppy. Eileen had wrapped him up in a box punched with airholes. When opening the box Emily had known there was something alive inside and just at the moment of undoing the box's lid, Cappy had given a delightful little yelp. With this image and sixteen years later, Emily lets out another such yelp. That was the noise the pup had made. Because of the unusual white marking which sat like a cap on top of his head, there'd never been any doubt in her mind what to call him. 'See his lovely eyes,' Eileen had said, kissing her. 'Just like yours. Wonderfully clear.'

In a way it would be better if he was knocked over by a car. A quick way to go, thinks Emily. And not the indignity of having to live in a tiny pen put up around the caravan. He would hate that. Just as long as he dies quickly and not in pain. Emily Egan veers so far into the middle of the road a car beeps at her loudly as she runs.

Baxter Tathra has taken the dog to the wharf where each day he fishes for danger. This day will be different from any other. The way his heart is battering at his rib cage tells him so, and the deep, almost black colour of the water. The whippet is tall and aloof, balancing his misery in silence as he sits on his bottom bones, looking for Emily. Every now and again he looks at Baxter as if he might solve the mystery of the morning after all.

'I'll put you out of your misery in just a mo,' says Baxter. He fiddles with the radio tuner and with his balls which, despite the cool wind coming off the water, seem to have swollen so large inside his jeans he curses his mother, feeling sure she has shrunk his Wranglers in a hot wash. He finds a song that suits his mood and turns it up. The whippet's ears fly backwards.

'Baby but you can't change that,' sings Baxter. The song still isn't finished when he takes the whippet outside and ties it up to the car. The dog stands, waiting more urgently for Emily now. His ears are strained forward, listening for her voice, even as Baxter takes out the five-hundred-dollar pistol he bought for killing sharks, and shoots the dog through its chest.

The wharf car park is empty of any vehicle except his own and, emboldened by the silence after the gunshot, Baxter puts the body on top of some plastic bags in the boot. He drives back through town to the club, where he loses steadily at the pokies until with his last dollar there is the mad rattle of coins. 'Yes!' he whoops with the thrill of the lucky omen and the buzz of his fourth rum and coke. Determined to set the rig up now rather than waiting until dark he drives back to the wharf. Still no one at the car park. 'Your luck holds, Baxter, your luck holds,' he says and opens up the boot. When he sees that blood has soaked through the plastic bags into the carpet of the boot, the voice of his mother complaining about steaks on the top rack of the fridge comes to him. She is always going on about that and now he sees what she means. Lucky the carpet is black, he thinks. The blood is dark on the red wool coat which he cuts off with his fishing knife. Then he puts the dog on the ground and, careful of his back, kneels beside it.

The large fishing hooks are hard to poke through the dead dog. It reminds him of some thin and inaccessible deep sea fish. Or of the thinnest school girls he finds passed out in the Woolworths car park on a Friday night. 'All fuckin' bones,' he says. He is still swearing at the whole elaborate apparatus he's set up to float off a ten-gallon drum, when he becomes aware of the family who have come to eat their lunch-time fish and chips at the wharf. Just one glare from him and they're making their hurried departure. 'No wucken forries,' he says to the dead dog's face. 'What are you looking at anyway,' he says and when the whippet's eyes won't close he puts hooks through them instead.

The wind seems to gather force then and even he feels shocked by the look of his bait. He slams the boot shut and begins to walk up the wharf. It is as if an afternoon southerly has blown up early, and he has to bend his head into the wind. He can feel the weight of the dog and is surprised it should be so heavy. He holds it away from his pale blue jeans. He is right at the edge of the wharf when he hears his name being called. It is Constable Richards, who got him the morning he drove over the bridge dragging a petrol bowser on the side of his car. Constable Richards is stepping out of his car and moving around to open up the passenger side of the door. 'Christ,' he says. 'Fucken fish 'n' chips family,' and with a big throw lets go of the rig. The dog and the drum float through the air like some bizarre airbrushed picture on the side of a panel van. He can't believe how slowly they travel before landing with a slap in the water. When he looks back Constable Richards is walking towards him and Emily Egan in her crocheted dress is like a bright triangular smudge staying at the end of the wharf. The water looks so sharky he could almost cry.

She knows she mustn't go up to the wharf where she has so often walked Cappy, to where the policeman is talking to Mrs Tathra's boy. Something terrible is up there. Emily Egan concentrates on a square of blue crocheted wool instead. She watches the way the wool has been hooked and joined, hooked and joined, and feels consoled by the knowledge of so many bobbles, so much pattern. She turns the hem of her dress over to feel the sea-valve-like patterns on the other side. If she'd known there was going to be this waiting time, she would've brought a hook to the wharf and a fresh ball of wool so that she could occupy her fingers. She strokes the lumps under the skin of her arm. Her hand falls down to where his head would normally be. The strangeness of not having his dear face. She walks around the police car to distract herself. The sight of his autumn coat in the gravel brings the first swell of tears. Her back feels like it is nearly breaking in two as she bends to take it into her fingers and, raising it to her face, smells his fresh blood.

'Sorry,' the undertaker had grunted, pushing Eileen into the green body bag, 'but there is nothing that can dignify this part of the process.' Zipping away her head last of all from sight. Cappy had come into the room and sniffed in a way that didn't recognise Eileen as Eileen. She was gone. Her face and her smell.

Eileen's family, with the same air of embarrassment they'd held for Eileen's tattoo, had asked Emily to move out of the cottage almost immediately. They wanted to sell, they said, ignoring all the years that Emily had lived with Eileen. In a burst of generosity, they offered the car. Yes, Emily could have Eileen's old red VW. She'd bought the caravan using the money from the car in this river town Eileen had always liked on their holidays north.

It is almost the end of the day when Mrs Tathra wakes up from the little blue tablet she took at lunch-time. As she drinks, she wipes away the water mark the glass has left on the kitchen counter using a blue sponge. In her house-slippers she tiptoes up the hall to his room. She can't remember if the door of his bedroom was open or shut. 'Baxter?' she says in her most persuasive tone of voice. 'Are you there Baxter?'

But when she pushes open the door with a pointed toe she sees that the room is undisturbed, that he hasn't been back since she hospital-tucked the sheets of his bed. It had taken her a long time to perfect a tight tuck on his water bed but she considers she's got the technique down pat now. She worries, as she always worries when she sees the bed, that one day it will fall through the floor. Emily Egan, looking up, will think then that miraculously she is seeing a waterfall cascading from underneath the footings of Mrs Tathra's immaculate mobile home.

In the hallway, she views for a moment or two the school portraits of Baxter. From Infants to his final year, she has them all. The flimsiness of the mobile home is apparent when her gaze falls down to the hole Baxter kicked through the wall in a temper. She had a pot-plant there for a while but it died. There is a darkness to the gap. The ragged shape makes Mrs Tathra feel that within her home, which she keeps so spic and span, is something unclean. She scans the photos again, looking for the year when the changes began.

Reluctantly, Mrs Tathra goes to her stool at the window to look down at Emily Egan's van. She still isn't home. The only movement comes from the white flutter of egrets settling briefly in the willow tree before lifting to fly down river like handkerchiefs in motion.

Even though the van looks as empty as it did this morning, Mrs Tathra persuades herself that at any moment the light will go on and that she'll see the face of Emily Egan tugging shut the curtains. Or that suddenly she'll appear standing with her whippet by the willow tree. In their crocheted garments they will appear as bright shapes of colour in the last light. The speedboats have left the river for the day and the quietness laps into Mrs Tathra in a way she can't stand. It must've been a hot day, she thinks, because when she unwraps a Cocktail Fruit it's sticky and tastes of plastic.

Mrs Tathra goes out onto her front porch with her pair of sewing scissors and unsnips her windchimes. Each time Baxter ties the windchimes it is as if with intent to strangle the life out of them.

There is just enough wind to make them dingle. The noise sets up a deeper disquiet and before she chokes on the boiled sweet she spits it into her hankie. The last line of poplar trees that give the park its name look like a competition advertisement, they are so golden in the late light. If you won that competition, thinks Mrs Tathra wistfully, you would be flown to Europe in the autumn with seven days' spending money.

Mrs Tathra's prosthesis has slipped during her sleep but she doesn't bother making it lie straight. She leans forward over her railing. Although she wouldn't be able to say for what it is she is hoping, she continues to stare down at Emily Egan's caravan. She thinks of the chicken she left on the small table, of the way the ants would run dark over its mauve bones and pale skin. If only, wishes Mrs Tathra, I'd popped it into the fridge for a poor old lady and her dog. She is standing waiting like this when Mr Johns appears from round the corner, holding her letter of complaint in his half opened hand.

Good. Oh good! she thinks and prepares her face, and puts her breast in place. It is suddenly quite clear. She would prefer, after all, to tear up that letter. Live and let live, Mr Johns, she gets ready to say. That's for the best, isn't it?

Burial

Allan **Donald**

Ulali Palmer lay with her legs drawn up, her face to one side, resting in the old Aboriginal woman's lap, a large, blood-soaked bath towel pressed between her thighs. She tried to focus on the young man leaning in the doorway. A soiled and threadbare Aboriginal flag hung above his curly black hair from a single crooked nail.

Her troubled eyes switched between the young man and the wet strip of floor that led from her bedroom to the couch where she lay.

Her mother had moved deftly as a poacher disposing of game as she retrieved the stillborn foetus and placenta, inspecting them for outward signs of abnormality before wrapping them separately in single bed sheets. It had taken her fifteen minutes to find the mop she seldom used. It had taken less than three minutes to clean the bloody mess from the floor, leaving a wet shining path, embellished with thin red swirls in the grime. She could have made an effort this time, the young woman thought, especially for a shame job like this.

Ulali looked at the young man once more. This time their eyes made contact. He stood with his arms folded, his upper body angled forward from the waist. Distractedly, he traced the cracks in the floor with his toe. His eyes shifted from the photograph glued to the wall above the couch, then back to Ulali and her broken-doll body, a wax image of the radiant young woman with her arms around him in the picture.

He'd spent most of the afternoon smoking yandi with his uncle. Heavily stoned and paranoid, he'd entered the house, terrified by the horrible cries of the women.

Believing at first he'd intruded on private womens' business, he stood petrified as Ulali walked towards him, wild-eyed and screaming, legs spread wide, arms out from her sides.

Awkward and stiff-legged in her fouled cotton frock, she'd left a gory trail spilling down like the discoloured water that often poured from the community's rusted taps. The old woman wailed as she gathered up the long purple cord with its dark red bundle attached. The tiny form slumped raw and glistening in her upturned palms, then slipped from her as she tried to pass it to her hysterical daughter.

Above the wailing he'd heard Ulali shouting, 'Hey, Calvin! Git outta here. Nana, help me Nana! Go on

Calvin. Git. This's got nothin t' do with you. Nothin for you t' see! Go on. Piss off!' Then, accompanied by even louder, more terrified screams, the placenta, like a large purple, black-veined slug, slithered from beneath her dress, dropping to the slippery floor with a slick smack. Looking wildly about, the bewildered, panic-stricken young man ran outside, clambered under the porch and hid.

Twenty minutes later, his face ashen, he staggered back into the doorway.

'You wanna go too, Calvin More! You black cunt! Fuckin molesterin my fuckin daughter! Ulali's only fourteen, remember. I trusted you. You dirty black cunt!' Bonnie Palmer started drinking early. By seven p.m. she was crying drunk and raving. Kicking over the kitchen chair, still holding the stubby in her hand, she strode towards her terrified daughter. Quickly the old black woman stood and blocked her way. Bonnie easily pushed the frail old grandmother aside and screamed at her cowering daughter, 'An' you too, you li'l slut! Oh! Yeah sure. We not doin' nothin, Mum,' the drunken woman mocked. 'We just kiss, that's all. Bull fuckin shit! Kiss alright an' poke too ay? Dirty li'l cunt! Musta been goin' on a while too, for 'im to get ya boontas like that!'

Shady Meadows, Ulali's stepfather, sat smoking on the dark porch, watching for the ambulance. Half an hour gone and still no sign of it. He looked at the young, dumbfounded man trembling in the doorway, but felt no sympathy. He was used to his de facto's star turns. Casually he flicked his cigarette over the rail; its glowing end embedded in the grey matted fur of Floyd, the family pet. The old dog raised his head from the grass and sniffed the air. Some random scratching dislodged the butt. Another quick scratch, a slower, more thoughtful clean of the genitals, and he swaggered under the porch.

Shady had complete control over Bonnie. It pleased him that with a simple show of kindness and some skilfully chosen words, he had achieved what Bonnie's husband, through years of physical and mental abuse, had not – total dominance. He'd discovered this power quite early in their relationship. It began when Bonnie was recovering from a final, vicious beating Ulali's father had given her. Shady had helped her through. Ever since then, even at her wildest, he could soothe her, and when alcoholic remorse threatened to push her over the edge, he could easily coax her back.

Shady pushed past the young man and once inside the house, made his way towards his stepdaughter. 'Leave the poor little bugger alone, woman.' He put his arms around the girl's shoulders and kissed the top of her head. She wrapped her arms around the handsome white man's waist as she knelt on the couch, sobbing. 'This girl's been through a lot. Poor kid couldn't even tell you she was six months gone cos she knows what you're like . . . and how come you didn't know she was pregnant anyway? Don't even know what's goin' on in your own fuckin home. So just lay off, fuck ya!'

He continued speaking more quietly now, gently hushing the constant interjections. With patience, he restored calm and soon the three women were sobbing quietly. Shady continued to hold Ulali. Bonnie hugged Nana Anna who in turn put her arm around her granddaughter.

Suddenly Calvin More screamed from the front porch, 'What you mob wanna b . . . blame me for? I don't know nuthink about no b . . . baby!' Everyone watched, stunned, as the normally quiet eighteen year old stormed out of the house.

The ambulance swung into the driveway, its head-lights sweeping the front of the dwelling like a searchlight. Still greatly distressed, Calvin decided to stay. Sitting on the fence, he watched as the paramedics, a man and a woman, got out. They walked towards the house, pulling on their latex gloves, their uniform black trousers hidden by the night, their shirts moving like white flags in the moonlight.

'Hello,' the woman called timorously.

'Go right in,' Calvin called from the darkness, with an authority that surprised him.

Combing his long blond hair with his fingers, Shady displayed himself in the doorway. He shook hands with the man and smiled at the woman. 'Patient's on the couch. Had a bit of a mishap, I'm afraid.'

The female paramedic, a plain-looking young woman, made her way purposefully towards Ulali.

The driver, a big, balding man in his forties, ambled in with an air of affected nonchalance, looking around at the damaged furnishings, smeared walls and dirty floor. He stared at Bonnie sitting at the old wooden table, strewn with empty bottles and cans. When she returned his stare, he smiled uncomfortably and knelt beside the young woman on the couch.

Bonnie ground her cigarette into the ashtray and opened another stubby, grunting in disgust.

Even on his knees, the medico loomed above Ulali. His gaze never left her as he considered her predicament. Ulali shifted uncomfortably, lowering her eyes as he fitted her with the oxygen mask while his partner applied surgical pads to stem the blood flow, clucking her tongue in dismay as she worked.

A few deep breaths of oxygen and Ulali was dreamily picking up fragments of the ambulance officer's conversation. 'Intra access . . . fluid drip . . . breathing not so rapid now . . . total miscarriage . . . poor kid . . .'

After the brief examination and treatment, the officers prepared Ulali for the trip to hospital. Shady, Bonnie and Nana Anna walked alongside the stretcher. Shady held the drip and Bonnie and Nana Anna offered assurances as they carried her out.

'That just about takes care of everything,' the driver said, to nobody in particular. Then, to test the link of solidarity with his partner, he added, 'What you reckon, Dot?' The woman smiled obligingly in reply.

Looking at Bonnie he said, 'You know we have to take everything with us. The pathologist will test her foetus separately and do some other tests on the placenta as well.'

Nana Anna moved with remarkable agility for an eighty year old. Quickly lifting the blanket from Ulali's feet, she gave a sigh of relief at seeing them both there, still firmly attached to her ankles.

Ulali looked up at her grandmother, shaking her head in disbelief. Pulling the old lady down to her she whispered, 'No Nana. Foetus. Foetus. He means the bubby.' She looked over at Calvin. He looked different somehow. For the first time he looked at her properly, like a real boyfriend.

'Excuse me, Mr ambulance man,' Bonnie said with slurred indignation, both hands on her hips. 'We take care of our own, thank you. I can take care of my own granddaughter's funeral thank you. We don't need you.'

'Fuck up, Bonnie. We can pick the baby up from the hospital later,' Shady said, pushing her towards the house. 'You're just making a cunt of yourself now. Just shut up, get inside and get to bed.'

Floyd sauntered into the kitchen, stopping three times to scratch behind his ear. Finally completing his ritualistic two and a half circular turns, he collapsed under the table at Shady's feet.

'Anyone fed this dog?' Shady asked through a garland of smoke rings. He sipped his coffee, not expecting a reply.

'I give him some Pal when I come back yesterday,' Ulali answered. 'But you know what kind, real fussy one, he turn his nose up at it.'

'He'll eat it when he's hungry, I s'pose,' Shady said. 'Prob'ly dig something up otherwise.' Then he added, 'What was the tucker like in hospital, honey?'

'Fuckin ugly, man. Real white fella shit. Ugh!' Ulali screwed up her face, sticking her finger down her throat in disgust. 'An' talk about shame-job, man. When I'm leavin they give me this li'l packet . . . silver, like inside a moselle cask, only it got zipper on it. I don' know what them big words they use. So I go to open it an' they go – "That's ya baby!" I didn't know. That's when I just wrapped her up in some bits o' rag 'n' shit an' brung her home . . . poor li'l thing.'

Shady cleared his throat, shifted in his chair and sipped his coffee.

Nana Anna picked her chipped green pannikin out of the dish-rack and poured the first of the day's many cups of tea. She took a couple of short, satisfying sips and, leaning against the sink, addressed the family. 'You mob gonna mek a track soon or what? Dat bubby gonna melt soon if you mob don' mek a track.' Pointing with her lips, and a quick upward movement of her head, towards the blue esky in the corner, containing the dead foetus.

'Still dunno whacha wanna bury li'l sister-girl on your grandfather's block for, Ulali,' Bonnie called from her bed, losing the struggle to sound reasonable. 'It'll take all fuckin day t' git there an' another day t' git back.'

Her head ached and her throat was dry. She'd polished off a cask of wine on her own last night. Today, she was determined not to drink. No. Not today. She was forty now. Where would she find another handsome, 27-year-old white man like Shady? No. Today she'd stay dry. Get back in his good books. One day off the grog wouldn't hurt.

Entering the kitchen, she was about to hug her daughter and tell her she understood why it was important for her to bury the baby close to her grandfather, when Shady turned on her. 'Jesus fuckin Christ, woman! Ya can't pull your fuckin head in for one fuckin day can ya?'

Bonnie quickly moved to his side and threw her arms around him. 'Sorry-sorry-sorry-shhh! Didn't mean it. Sorry-shh! I'm crook from the grog, that's all.' While she spoke she kissed him loudly and repeatedly on the mouth.

She pinched his cheeks and tilted his head from side to side; smiling seductively at him, she said, 'Shady got deadly eyes. Don' you reckon Ulali?'

'Alright I s'pose.' Ulali shrugged, looking down at the table.

The old lady liked Shady. He didn't hit her daughter. Her face aglow, giggling she said, 'You look, Ulali! Your mum jus' lovin Shady up real good way now, you look!'

'She just gammon, Nana . . . a real cupboard lover. You watch, when his back turned, she'll just run 'im down to the lowest, you watch.'

Everyone laughed and although Ulali smiled as she spoke, Bonnie detected an edge of defiance in her daughter's words she'd never encountered before.

Beneath the only shade tree in the yard, Nana Anna sat on an old car seat which years ago had been dumped against its gnarled and tattooed trunk. Taking in their every movement and gesture, she watched the family load the ute for the bush trip. At her feet Floyd stretched and yawned. She lit her crab-claw pipe, drew deeply on it, raised one buttock and farted. Floyd shook his head vigorously and moved under the porch. The old woman watched, detached, as he moved away. She saw Calvin coming long before the others did but said nothing.

Shady lived his life in constant dread of appearing foolish. He was completely unable to accept responsibility for even the most trivial mistake. Distracted by Calvin's unexpected arrival, he accidentally poured water from the ute's radiator onto the speeding fan. Instantly he blamed a faulty hose connection. In an effort to draw attention from himself, he bent down sideways to Bonnie and whispered in cruel imitation, 'C . . . Calvin's c . . . c . . . coming. Say g . . . g . . . good morning to your son-in-law.'

Bonnie ignored Shady and, hands on hips, glared menacingly at Calvin. Shady found her harder to control sober. Uneasily, he turned the shut-off nozzle on the hose and stood behind her.

'Fuck off Calvin!' she said, her voice quavering. 'You caused enough trouble round 'ere.'

Shamefaced, Calvin ignored Bonnie and, dropping the bike, sat beside Nana Anna. She moved slightly to make room for him although there was plenty. 'No good lookin sad. You mek me shame, you!' Nana Anna chided. 'You prop'ly no good, you!'

Calvin looked at the old woman, tears in his eyes, the palms of his hands upturned towards her. 'B . . . But I didn't do nuthink.'

Nana Anna cuffed him hard around the ear. 'Don' tell liar you stinking dawg!'

Calvin let out a loud, stressful 'Yukai!' and got to his feet.

Ulali had been inside putting on her shoes and on hearing the argument, came onto the porch. 'It's okay, Nan,' she said calmly. 'Come inside, Calvin.'

'No fuckin way mate!' Bonnie shouted, moving towards the porch. 'I don' want that dirty stinkin prick nowhere near my home!'

Ulali stamped her foot and whined in protest.

Calvin looked up at Ulali. It was the first time she'd spoken to him since the miscarriage. Even when he visited her in hospital she'd refused to speak, leaving him hurt and more confused than before.

He was about to speak to her when Shady intervened.

'Listen you mob. Let's get the burial out of the way, then we'll all sit down and sort this whole thing out.' He spoke with an uncharacteristic nervousness that took everyone off guard.

Bonnie was silent for a moment, then spoke through gritted teeth. 'Excuse me, but no dirty childmolestin dawg's comin to my granddaughter's funeral. Thank you very much.'

Shady took her by the arm and led her away. 'Look,' he said, trying to calm her. 'Poor bugger does have a right to be there you know. I mean . . . fuckin hell, Bonnie, he does have a right.'

Bonnie looked at Shady, listening intently as he spoke. As usual, she gave in to him. 'Okay. He can come, but he's sittin on his own in the back.'

'Alright, he's sittin in the back for Christ's sake.' Shady rolled up the hose as he walked towards Nana Anna. 'You comin, Mum?' he asked politely.

'No more, good boy,' she said, waving him away with her pipe. 'No more. You go.'

Some time ago she was involved in a single vehicle roll over, leaving one countryman dead and three others including herself badly injured. These days, she flatly refused to travel by road. Not going to the funeral would cause her pain but she would make amends with the ceremonial smoking of the home.

'It gonna rain. You an' Floyd cover up wid dis.' Nana Anna gave Calvin a large sheet of orange plastic as he and the dog waited on the back of the ute.

'It's not gonna rain, olgamin,' Calvin replied, accepting the cover with a broad smile.

'It gonna rain. Take it.' This time she reinforced her warning with a light rap on his knee. He smiled once more, shaking his head.

Two hours out and Bonnie's resolve not to drink was worn away by the relentless rain and the monotonous rub of the windscreen wipers. 'Stop at the next servo. I need a drink.' She turned as she spoke, checking out Calvin and the dog. 'Floyd's gettin wet poor thing . . . you look.'

'What about Calvin? Poor bloke,' Shady said, glancing back quickly then lighting a smoke.

'Ah fuck him!' Bonnie spat the words from her mouth. 'It's me fuckin dawg I'm worried about.'

About an hour before dawn next day, they reached the derelict weekender Ulali's grandfather had built back in the seventies. Ulali chose a spot near her grandfather's grave to bury her daughter.

The rain stopped and Bonnie kept drinking. 'Li'l sister-girl's still got no name ya know. Have ta call her somethin my girl. Can't just bury her like that with no name,' she spoke ruefully, looking down at the red soil of the grave site.

'I thought sister-girl was her name . . . that's what everyone keeps calling her anyway.' Ulali's eyes gleamed with tears. 'It's a nice name . . . Sister-girl . . . always loved that name.'

'Alright then sister-girl, Sister-girl it is.' Mother and daughter embraced, laughing quietly.

Shady finished digging away the clumps of red soil just on daybreak and gently placed the tiny swaddled corpse in the grave. Bonnie waited until he'd covered Sister-girl's body before opening her Bible.

'Everyone ready? Okay.' She cleared her throat and in a trembling voice, began reading aloud. 'My grief is beyond healing . . .'

She looked up as Shady moved closer to Ulali, placing one arm around her shoulders, taking her right hand in his. Bonnie's gaze shifted to Calvin, standing on the outer, trying his hardest to look solemn. She cleared her throat once more. 'My heart is sick within me . . .'

Shady sobbed as Ulali let go a whimper. Bonnie went quiet, her hands shaking. The page blurred with tears, she continued. 'Hark to the cry of the daughter of my people . . .'

Ulali cried aloud and threw her arms around Shady's neck. He returned her embrace, his eyes on Bonnie. His pride relenting to a pitiful, futile pleading he said, 'Listen Bonnie, there's something . . .'

Bonnie's throat tightened. Her face flushed, she kept reading aloud. 'Um . . . from the length of the land . . . oh shit . . . the length and breadth of the land . . . oh you bastard!'

She flung the Bible at Shady's feet and, sobbing uncontrollably, staggered towards the wooden bench beside the water tank. Rummaging inside the torn carton, she pulled out a can of beer, reefed it open and emptied it inside her. By the time she'd opened another, Calvin was sitting on the opposite end of the bench.

'What the fuck's goin' on, Calvin?' Bonnie growled through her tears, her words seething in her spittle. 'Is somethin goin' on with them pair o' cunts?'

'They been kai-ai for one an . . . an . . . another for the longest time now.' Fed up, he added, 'That's what I . . . I . . . I been tryin to tell you mob for a . . . a . . . ages.'

Bonnie sighed. 'So it's his kid then.' She looked through the doorway of the crumbling building to where Ulali and Shady sat in earnest conversation at a rickety wooden table. 'Look at 'em will ya? The happy fuckin couple.' She lit a cigarette and shuddered at its effects.

'I think it m . . . must be his. It's not mine. She wouldn't let me touch her. Reckoned no . . . no . . . nobody has. She gammon told me she was still a vir . . . vir . . . vir–'

Bonnie got up and began searching the long grass around the water tank. Calvin eyed her suspiciously, still trying to finish his sentence. He persevered, his jaw vibrating. Bonnie picked up an axe and the last stubborn syllable came roaring out.

'–gin! Are you crazy? You'll kill him with that!' He jumped up and wrested the axe from her.

Not missing a beat, Bonnie looked around for something else to help her vent her anger and disgust. She found a slender ironwood limb about two metres in length and quite heavy.

'That's more like it Missus P,' Calvin said, grinning. Enthusiastically he joined in the march towards the rotten mongrel who had stolen his girl. A sudden downpour caught them midway and they broke into a trot.

Bonnie loped inside the shack, wielding her club. Shady looked up at her, his eyes wide, mouth open.

He folded his arms over his head and leaned away from her. Calvin's sadistic grin vanished as Bonnie brought the heavy ironwood whistling across her daughter's unprotected back. The loud hollow thud pulsed through Ulali's head. The pain was instant and unbearable. She jerked upright, helplessly shrugging her shoulders. Unable to breathe, her face twisted in agony, she collapsed unconscious.

'Wanna open ya legs for *my* man do ya, ay cunty?' Bonnie screamed, raising the club again.

Calvin moved quickly. Grabbing the piece of wood, he twisted it backwards over her head, wrenching it out of her grasp. He felt something soft give at the jagged end of the timber. Behind him, Shady yelped then groaned. Calvin swung around, saw Shady stumbling about in a crazy high-stepping motion, crying and cursing Bonnie, his right eye hanging off the ridge of his cheek.

Calvin bent over Ulali, cradled her in his arms, frantically puffing his mouth on hers, trying to revive her.

Rain pelted the tin roof beneath a roll of thunder. Floyd wandered in and curled up under the table, his legs and belly splattered with red, freshly turned earth. He got unsteadily to his feet once more. Arching his back and lowering his head, he hawked loudly, bringing up a tiny bone and gristle. Nobody noticed. Smacking his jowls with long laps of his tongue he yawned and went to sleep.

The Night of the Fruit-Pickers

Margaret **Simons**

When Rita Phipps did the washing up she always finished by plunging the clean cutlery in boiling water from the kettle. It satisfied her to do a thorough job. No germs survived her efforts.

Rita Phipps also had regular conversations with God. Mostly, the conversations took place at night, and were about Rita's husband, Ed.

Rita and Ed were good people. They were involved in good works in the town of Newera. Rita organised the community teas. She ran fundraising raffles. She visited the elderly in hospital. All of these things took place during the day. Good works for women did not extend past dark.

Ed was the president of Rotary. He was on the council. He worked on their fruit block during the day, and at night he took the car and drove into town for meetings. Ed was hardly ever at home.

After the meetings, Ed would stay on at the pub for a couple of beers. When Rita suggested he come home early, Ed told her that the most important business was conducted after the meeting. 'That's when you lobby,' he said, 'over a few sherbets. That's when you find out what people really think.'

Rita did not take alcohol.

Rita took tea out of porcelain cups with her women friends. You could tell the cups were porcelain. If, when washing up, she held them up to the window, she could see the light through them. This was a measure of their fineness.

Rita said to her friends: 'I lie at night and I say to God, "You know Ed should be here beside me, God. You know that".' Rita, porcelain cup in hand, looked up while saying this, her head on one side. She looked as though she were talking to a parrot suspended in a cage overhead. She looked as though she were trying to charm it into saying, 'hello'. With her free hand, she patted the air beside her, as though patting the empty side of her bed.

'You know, God, he should be here beside me.'

At night, when Ed had taken the car into town, the house was mute. It was utterly silent.

The house was in the middle of the block, and surrounded by neat rows of rigid, shiny-leaved citrus trees that hardly moved with the breeze. When they did move, the leaves didn't rustle but slid over each other in a formal sort of way, like a handshake.

In summer, just before midnight, there would be a noise. The automatic sprinkler system that kept the lawn green would come on. Watering at night was the only way grass could be kept alive through the heat. During the day the droplets either dried up before they could soak in, or else they rested on the leaves and focused the sun.

Newera sat in the middle of the great South Australian plain that ran without a break into the desert. Only the river made life possible, and the river could not be seen. It was sunk between cliffs, not meant to be noticed. Newera was flat. In summer it was easy to believe the hole in the ozone layer was right overhead and there was nothing to protect the people who crawled across the red sand and drove along the snakes of bitumen road. Naked sun and deep space, and Rita and Ed doing all the good works without which Newera would . . . would have lapsed. Would not have been what it was.

So in summer there was the hissing of the sprinklers for an hour or two, then deep silence. It was now, in the silence, that Rita and God conversed. After they had finished their conversation, Rita would drop off to sleep, then she would wake and hear the car coming, rounding the bend in the dirt road. The headlights would sweep the wall. She waited for the slam of the car door. Then he was in the room, taking it over with his preparations for bed. Ed came into the silence not knowing it had been there. The silence was Rita's secret, but she always told Ed what God had said.

'God spoke to me tonight,' she said to him one night in the post-midnight hours, just as he crawled under the sheets.

'Praise the Lord,' he said. Rita looked at him.

'He said you should come to more of the community teas. You are getting a reputation as a person . . . as the sort of person . . .'

'What?'

God had been eloquent, but Rita had lost the words.

'As the sort of man who doesn't come to community teas.'

'Ah.'

'As the sort of man who stays in the pub.'

'Ah.' Ed fell asleep.

Now was one of the times of year when Rita's silence was disturbed. It was the grape-picking season. The fruit-pickers would arrive the next day.

Rita's lawn petered out into a red sand apron. On the other side of the apron was the fruit-pickers' cottage, then a walnut tree, then the chook shed full of strutting, cold-eyed birds, then the silent rows of glossy trees.

The fruit-pickers were coming.

When the fruit-pickers were in town the locals locked their car doors when they parked in the main street. The rest of the year leaving your car open was a sign of belonging. It proved that you trusted everyone – even the people you couldn't stand.

The fruit-pickers sat on the steps of the pub and watched, not caring what the town thought of them. Fruit-pickers had wild blue eyes. The men had muscles and tattoos. The women wore singlets and drank from the bottle. Or they wore cotton dresses that you could see through.

Working, they would strip the trees, then call in to the back door of the house to ask for a couple of dollars advance on their pay. They had no money. There was no substance to them.

Fruit-pickers arrived in summer, when the air smelt so dry it tickled your nose. They picked the grapes through the night under fluorescent lights, getting them at their sweetest, and avoiding the heat. They snored through the morning. They went to the pub in the afternoon.

With the new year, they switched to working days to get the stone fruit, and in the evening they sat on the verandahs of the fruit-picking cottages, or even on the steps of the pub, and rolled their own cigarettes. The smoke from the cigarettes did not smell like tobacco, but Newera at these times of year had no sense of smell.

You could not arrest a fruit-picker. Once, many years ago, when Rita was a girl there had been an argument, and the fruit-pickers had left Newera in the middle of summer. Children were taken out of school. Families worked without taking time to sleep, but still the grapes turned to sultanas on the vines, and the apricots rotted on the trees.

You could not be nasty to a fruit-picker. You could not control them. You just hoped – that they would control themselves.

With the apricots, the men picked and the women stood on concrete floors in corrugated iron sheds, cutting the apricots in half for drying, laying them out on trays, putting the trays in the sun, stacking them and smoking them with sulphur. If you ate dried apricots too soon after the smoking, they made you fart, and the farts smelt of the sulphur smoke. The fruit-pickers ate lots of apricots. They lay about in the early evening on the verandah of the fruit-pickers' cottage, within shouting distance of Rita's lawn. They lay about farting and laughing at each other's smell.

God congratulated Rita on her endurance.

When the stone fruit was finished, the fruit-pickers disappeared, but they came again in winter for the citrus, wearing checked cotton shirts with grimy sleeves, stripping the trees of their little balls of winter sun. Then, before spring, they were gone again.

When the fruit-pickers were in town, Newera was different. Normally the people drinking in the Newera Club knew who they were, and where they belonged. They knew they were not the Aborigines drinking down by the river. Nor were they the people gathered in the front bar of the hotel. 'Members and Guests Only', said the sign over the entrance to the Newera Club. Some people were never members, and the guests were all so regular one wondered why they didn't join. But when the fruit-pickers were in town, the guests signed themselves in with extra care. Some of them even joined.

The fruit-pickers were loud. They couldn't care less. But when it came to the trees and the vines, their fingers plucked so delicately the trees hardly moved. They held the fruit in grimy palms, and never bruised it. The women cut apricots so fast you couldn't see the movement of the knife. A dollar a tray, Ed paid them, and the only way you could make it worthwhile was to do fifty or more trays a day.

Four hundred apricot halves per tray. Ed made sure they packed them close. The mushy ones went on the edge, so they could be scraped off and made into the stuff that went into the centre of chocolates. The women's feet swelled from standing on the concrete, and the apricot stones lay all around – ankle deep at lunch-time. Calf deep by night.

Ed had long ago stopped giving work to the university students. They damaged the trees, took up too much room in the cutting shed, and were too slow. 'I'm not a charity,' Ed said. Rita, who ran most of Newera's charities, was forced to agree.

There once had been a different sort of picker. For years there had been Phyllis and Reg, a retired couple with their own neat little caravan, camping stove and folding chairs. Their retirement hobby was to follow the fruit around the nation. Phyllis wore cotton dresses and a straw hat. Reg wore proper shorts and long socks. Phyllis and Reg were self-sufficient, and did not use the fruit-pickers' cottage, or mix with what Phyllis described, talking to Rita, as 'that kick-your-heels-on-the-steps-of-the-pub sort of person'. But two seasons before, Reg and Phyllis had been too slow. Now they didn't come any more.

When the fruit-pickers were in town, Rita thought about change. She thought about how the young people – her own children, born before she had any idea of what children meant – had left. She thought about how old she felt, although she was only middle-aged. For most of the year, Newera and Rita were safe in their habits. Newera and Rita trusted themselves. But when there were fruit-pickers in the cottage across the way, on the steps of the pub, not caring what anyone thought, Newera felt affronted. Newera felt itself challenged. Newera felt self-righteous. Rita plunged the cutlery into the boiling water, and reminded herself of who she was.

They began arriving early the next afternoon. Ed saw to them. Men in jeans, women in jeans and singlets or in soft, floating cotton dresses. They did their washing and hung it out on the length of string between the trees at the back of the cottage. They wandered around with bottles or cups of tea in their hands. They slept.

In the early evening, Ed drove into town. Rita shut the chooks into the shed. Ed had made it safe from foxes. He had buried barbed wire under the soil to spike their scrabbling paws and tender noses. Now the chooks were preparing for sleep – fluffing themselves up, shitting their watery shits.

Outside the shadows were growing in their ruthless, silent way. At this time of year the sunsets were red.

For the last five minutes of light, the shadows changed from grey to deep, engorged colors, and there wasn't a sound except for the sound of Rita's flat leather heels on the sand.

Then there was a sound. A motorbike approaching. It rounded the corner, threw up the dust, and stopped. The rider had thin legs – like pipe cleaners – and his jeans fitted them so neatly you could almost overlook how dirty they were. He had a leather jacket on. Rita could see the holes in the silk lining as he unzipped it, and his chest inside the shirt was lean and hard, and the hair he shook out of the helmet was longer than it should have been.

Rita felt herself firming. All the softness of her solitary day was leaving her now. Her firmness took the form of a resolve to be charitable. She walked over to the bike just as he dismounted. He was a little shorter than her. There was no softness about him anywhere. He was all sinew and tight-drawn flesh.

'Miss,' he said.
'Are you one of the pickers?'
'You got it.'
'You're the last to arrive. My husband . . . my husband won't be back until late tonight, but I can show you where you're staying.'

'Right.' He turned and unhooked the octopus straps that were holding a bag to the back of the bike, and swung the bag over his shoulder.

'Is that all your things?'

'Yep. I travel light.' He grinned at her. His smile had an astonishing effect. It changed his face. He actually looked like a different person – a nicer person, she decided. She gave him a little smile back, and wondered how he had ended up a fruit-picker.

She walked with him over to the cottage, and showed him into the dormitory with its rows of single beds. Several of the pickers had taken the mattresses off their wire bases and put them together on the ground, to make double beds. Everyone was asleep, and the room was heavy with the sound of their breathing. The motorcyclist swung his bag onto the vacant bed and crept out, exaggerating his tiptoeing and smiling that smile. 'Is there somewhere I can take a shower?'

'Outside the back door. Turn left.'

'Could I borrow a towel? Just for tonight.'

He came over to her later to return the towel. He was washed and sweet-smelling. He had put on clean jeans and a white T-shirt and his hair was silky now, and held back in a pony tail. Rita was making herself a cup of tea. The kitchen furniture, nothing factory-made, glowed and was solid. Rita felt firm. Charitable. She could afford to be kind.

He looked at the pot, the steam rising out of its spout.

'Arrived at the right time, did I?'

'Well. It looks like it, doesn't it?'

She rested her hands on the wooden table – the same kitchen table her mother had used, and that she had done her homework on. The kitchen table told her she was safe against him. Nothing would change in her life. Nothing would change.

She wanted him to see her like this. Poor boy. She wanted him to understand what it was that he was missing out on, with his shiftless life. Rita Phipps, she thought to herself. I am Rita Phipps, and this is my kitchen.

He pulled a chair out from under the table. She could see the tendons on his wrist – like the tendons in one of her chickens when she was preparing it for the pot. Hard and slippery. Standing out when you flexed the joint. She gave him a mug in the shape of an owl. He held it between cupped hands, and he smiled at her again.

It was dark outside now, and she could hear the other fruit-pickers. They were waking up. She heard the pump cutting in to bring up water from the river for their showers. She heard the vague clatter of saucepans.

'Have you lived here long?' he asked.

'All my life.' I am fixed. I am solid. I am Rita Phipps.

'And your hubbie?'

'His life too. And you? Where do you come from?'

He grinned a thin-lipped grin. His smiling mouth was like a segment cut from an orange.

'I come from all over. I come from the ether.'

She began to chop an onion, wondering what to say. For the first time she feared that he, like her children, was thinking of her in a mocking fashion. That later, out of earshot, he would tell jokes about her.

'I come from everywhere and nowhere,' he said.

'So you have no home?' She was trying to get back on the front foot.

'No home. No ties.' That smile again. 'A free spirit.'

Rita glanced out the window, thinking to read the registration plates on his bike. He must come from *somewhere*, but although she knew the motorbike was there, the night had crept down on them and she couldn't see it. The window was no longer something that could be looked through. It was just a square of hard nothingness on the wall.

'But you have a name, I suppose?' She asked the question grudgingly. Why did it seem as though he was in control, and she was the one seeking, wanting?

He stretched back in the chair. His shirt came untucked with the stretch and she could see his waist, and the taut space below; the thimble belly button and the beginning of hard, bony pelvis.

Rita turned back to her onion. What if he were crazy? She felt her breath coming a little sharper. If she called out . . . the fruit-pickers would hear her, but would they come?

'Your name?' she said again, slicing the onion with hard little movements.

He stood up and came over. Together they looked down at the onion. For the first time in thirty years, Rita's hand slipped and she cut into her nail, and into the flesh beneath. She dropped the knife and brought her thumb up to her mouth, and stood there for a moment, sucking.

'My name,' he said, 'is Rape.'

She bit her thumb. She must have misheard. Surely.

'Ray?' she ventured, over her thumb.

'That's right.'

She turned away from him and rummaged in a drawer for Elastoplast. The drop of blood that had fallen from her thumb was sinking into the cut surface of the onion. She threw it away and took another from the string bag hanging just inside the pantry door.

'Ray,' she said. I should tell him to go, she thought. But she still hadn't won her victory. There was no wistfulness in him. No sign that he appreciated the hot tea, and the solidity of the furniture, and the owl-shaped mug, and the fact that an evening meal was being cooked, but not for him.

He was a bad sort, she said to herself. Rita was like a lover in a bad mood. She wanted to be angry with him, to mark out the separation between them, yet at the same time she did not want him to leave. Watch me, even when I am angry with you. Like me, even when I don't like you. Tell me who I am. That I matter.

'Do you get lonely out here?' he asked.

'Busy. I keep very busy. And it is a good community.'

Ray got up, walked to the sink and gazed at the plug hole.

'It's a community that just takes you to its heart,' she said.

'I'd better go.'

'That makes you feel you belong.'

'I'd best be going.'

'Well. Yes. Ed will be here tomorrow. He'll show you what to do.'

'And you. Will I see you tomorrow?'

'Quite possibly. Not that it matters.'

He waved a hand, and pushed open the screen door. It fell back after him, bouncing against the door jamb. He had let in the mosquitoes. Rita got the fly spray, and shot them down. Their bodies, when they fell to the floor, were too small to see.

Rita was getting ready for bed when it happened, undressing, as always, in the dark. She was just about to pull her blouse over her head when she heard a footfall on the verandah outside her bedroom window. She looked up, arms crossed over her chest, grasping the hem of the blouse. There, like a spider against the window, was the silhouette of a man.

Rita felt – actually felt – the adrenalin release itself into her blood, but she did not, could not move. The house was old and wooden. The window was open. There was only a fly screen between her and him. If she moved suddenly, he would hear. He would know she was there.

She stood there for minutes. The body against the window was sagging inwards now, as though the person were tired and leaning against the house, or as though he was trying to peer into the darkness.

Rita moved towards the door, not tiptoeing, but trying not to touch the ground at all. She tried to glide. She reached the door. Behind her there was a bang, as though a vase had been knocked from the windowsill. She didn't look back. She ran light-footed through the kitchen, opened the back door, let it fall closed behind her, and ran off into the night where, she knew, the dark was so impenetrable that she could not be found.

Only when you get out of reach of electric light do you realise how very dark the night can be. There was no moon. Rita brought her hand up in front of her face, and could not see it. Nor could she see the dirt track she wanted to follow. I will feel my way, she told herself. It turns a little just here – and suddenly her shoes were full of red sand and her face was being scratched by the branches of the stiff little lemon trees. Such cruel thorns they had, under their shiny leaves.

She struck out to the left again, and knew she had found the middle of the road because it was harder. She tipped the sand out of her shoes, standing on one leg to do it. She had always had a good sense of balance. Then she walked on, feeling with her feet for the firmer sand of the road. But her shoes allowed her no sense of where she was. She took them off. Then, looking behind her to make sure no one was watching (although she could not even see her own feet), she took off her support stockings. Rita wore support stockings even in summer, because she was rarely off her feet. They reduced her legs to pillars of uniform colour. They hid the pathos of the ankle bone. Now, barefoot for the first time in years, she could *feel* the road between her toes. She could make out the compacted tyre marks and the soft churned-up bit in the middle, and the weeds on either side.

She could have shut her eyes and been no less able to find her way. She looked up at the stars, and walked ahead with her shoes and stockings in one hand. The stars were very colourful. How wrong it was to think of them as white. She saw pink and green and icy blue and great swathes of pastel galaxies, like cirrus clouds, above them.

She walked on, sensing the whole world through her toes. She felt proud now, though her heart was beating with the upset and panic of it all. Nobody could see her here, and, if she told people about this night-time walk, nobody would be able to imagine how it had been – how very dark it had been. It was too dark for her to be seen, even in the imagination. People hearing the story would imagine her moving in the spotlight of their minds. They would not imagine it dark enough, or her sufficiently alone.

Rita felt the itching in her nose that told her she was about to cry, but now she was close enough to the highway to catch glimpses of headlights making corridors of white on the great black plane. She could hear the roar of the cars and the bellowing of the trucks. They were rushing past the entrance to the block without a thought for her, a woman so used to the dark now that it would not have surprised her if her clothes and face had been stained black by the air.

She was at the highway. The next car that came along would catch her in its lights. Rita put on her stockings and shoes. A truck rounded the corner, and a giant shadow of Rita was thrown down the tunnel of road. Rita stepped out and waved her arms, and the truck braked and stopped, the various parts of it huffing and wheezing and letting off pressure, and the driver leaned out, sweaty and pear-shaped in a singlet. 'Yep?' he said, and when she took a moment to reply, the annoyance left his face, and he got down from his high seat and put an arm around her shoulders.

'There, love. There. Where have you come from? What's your name?'

Trucks did not normally go right into the town. Normally they thundered along the by-pass, not even acknowledging that there *was* a town. But the truck driver took Rita all the way into the pub, and the noise was so loud it disturbed the drinkers who had gathered there after the Rotary meeting, and they came out and stood on the verandah to watch. Rita climbed down from the cabin, like Jonah emerging from the whale, and the truck gasped, gathered itself, and, like a vast animal, made its way around the roundabout and back off up the hill.

'Mrs Phipps!' the drinkers on the verandah said, and looked at each other.
'Where's Ed?' she asked, and only understood later about the silence. One of them nodded towards the ladies lounge. Rita walked through and there he was, sitting with the fruit-picker women, one of them on his lap. His head was thrown back, laughing. When his head came forward, he saw Rita.

'Ah.'

Rita could find nothing to say. 'I was frightened,' she began. 'One of the pickers . . .' The fruit-picker woman on Ed's lap looked at her, smiling. Rita began to cry.

They drove back together. Halfway home, Rita broke the silence.

'Don't you think you owe me an explanation?'

'It was nothing. Just some fun.'

'But with . . . *her*. How could you. Don't you ever think of me . . . on my own?'

'We've been through this before.'

'We have never been through this before.'

Silence.

At last Ed said again: 'Really, it was nothing. A few sherbets. Bit of fun.'

Rita was crying again. Just a bit of fun, and anything could have happened to her.

Ed went into the house first, searched every room, and found nothing. No sign of disturbance. No sign that there ever had been a silhouetted man against the window. That night, Rita wore a winter nightie, and with it, cotton underpants.

In the morning she looked out of the window and saw Ed talking to the fruit-pickers. Ray was there, looking faded and small in the morning light. While Rita watched he put out one arm, tendons standing out, and pulled one of the batik girls into the curve of his waist and hip.

Ed came in. 'Ray. He's the one?' he said.

'Yes.'

'I thought you said he hadn't been here before.'

'*I've* never seen him.'

'He was here for the citrus last winter,' Ed said.

'No.'

'Good worker. You're sure it was him?'

'Who else would it have been?'

'Ah.'

That night, Ed didn't go out. He made recompense and stayed at home. He fell asleep in his armchair. Rita walked out into the warmth and the dark. She was invisible now. She was someone else.

She walked around the house, looking through the lounge-room windows at Ed, feeling the strangeness of seeing him there, hairy and small, helpless in sleep. Looking at him from the outside now, she didn't have to . . . care.

Then Rita walked further out, into the darkness, and towards the island of electric light of the fruit-pickers' cottage.

They had left all the lights on. Wasteful. Rita remembered her own voice, and her mother's voice before that, years ago, talking to the children. 'We're not made of money,' she used to say, every time they left a room without flicking the switch.

Now she walked around peering through the windows, seeing the fruit-pickers. In the kitchen a woman was holding a spoon in her long, fruit-picker fingers, and stirring a mixture on the stove. She was talking at the same time, smiling, making faces. Everyone in the room laughed with her.

Rita moved further round the house. This was the sitting-room. She felt like a scientist or a child, looking at animals through a one-way mirror. It was as though the fruit-pickers were ants in a glass ant-farm.

Here they were lolling around on the floor and on Rita's old settee that she had consigned to the fruit-pickers' cottage five years before. The women were leaning against the men, cuddling into their armpits. Rita could almost smell those sweaty armpits through the glass, feel the damp heat of the bodies. The fruit-pickers had their eyes half closed. There was music playing on a tape-deck, but Rita couldn't hear it.

Rita found Ray lying on his bed in a room on his own. Rita came closer. She stood with her hands spread out against the glass, seeing the little clouds of moisture spread out around her fingertips. Her mouth was open. She was breathing heavily, and her breath came and went on the glass. Obscuring Ray, revealing Ray.

Rita sagged against the window. She ached to be inside, now. She ached to be – someone other than Rita Phipps.

Ray did not open his eyes to see her.

End of the Road

Ann **Dombroski**

Old Dickie Shepherd pulled hard but the hose came no further. He looked back along its length which stretched straight and taut through the tomato patch. He shifted his weight onto his shorter leg. The hose used to reach all the way to the mandarin tree.

The back door slammed and he heard June calling his name. His wife appeared, breathless, in her red swimmers. 'The telly's gone.' Dickie gave the hose a final tug and dropped it in the dirt. Water spewed over the strawberry patch. 'How do you mean?'

But she was off again, ducking under the grapevine. Dickie hobbled up to the house. Things disappearing. He went into the lounge-room and stared at the black face of their new large Sony. 'Not that one,' June said from the doorway. 'The little bloke.'

In their bedroom he saw the empty space on the chest of drawers. 'What else?'

'Nothing, as far as I can see.' June slid the cupboard shut.

'Just it.' He stared bitterly at the empty spot.

At tea-time Dickie said to his grandson, 'We had a bit of a robbery this afternoon.'

'Yeah?' Craig's eyelids were pressing down.

'The portable TV was nicked.' Dickie folded a slice of bread and bit into it. He glanced at June, who was dishing up baked pumpkin at the bench. Craig's head rolled into a nod, and then kept on nodding to some internal rhythm.

'That telly was your grandfather's retirement present.' June knocked the gravy spoon against the pan.

'Yeah?' Craig pushed up an eyebrow.

Dickie moved the vase of roses aside and pushed the bread towards him. 'I haven't spoken to the police yet. And I won't have to, if the telly turns up.' A silly smile floated across Craig's lips as he peeled off three slices.

'He's on the pot again,' Dickie said to June after dinner. He rattled the cutlery in the sink. 'Lost in bloody space.'

'He'll hear you.'

Dickie looked into the lounge-room and saw Craig smiling at nothing funny on TV. He shook his head. 'When's his next shot?'

'Tomorrow.'

'Not a day too soon.'

When Dickie next turned round, Craig was standing in the kitchen. 'I'm goin' up to Sharon's.' His eyelids falling down.

'Bit late, isn't it?'

Craig's eyes focused on the clock. 'It's only eight o'clock, Grandad.'

Dickie wiped down the side of the bench where gravy had spilled. He heard Craig ask June for a lend of ten bucks, just till his cheque came, and saw June pull a twenty from her purse. Craig gave her a hug, and sneaked a rose from the vase on his way out the door.

The community nurse had a lumpish body in a tight uniform. Dickie sat with her at the plastic table on the lawn. He watched her shake out a large handkerchief and blow her nose, making a hooting sound like a man. Behind her, his wife's pink bloomers drifted round on the clothesline.

The nurse said, 'I don't think he's going to show.'

Dickie nodded. 'He's shot through for the day.'

'Well, I'll just keep coming back till I catch him.' She hooked the strap of her stiff leather bag over her shoulder but then unhooked it again as June came down the steps in her white bowling dress, a plate of sultana scones and pots of jam and butter sliding on the tray. Dickie looked at the scones which sat heavily on the plate. Over the years, June's scones had got denser and flatter. Nevertheless, he, like the nurse, opened one out and inside, the scone was warm and hungry for butter.

'Craig hates the Modicate,' June said, pulling up a plastic chair.

'They all do.'

'He says it's like walking through porridge.'

The nurse smiled.

Dickie ate another scone, staring at the clean white line the hem of June's dress made across her tanned knees.

'He won't tell anyone he's on a special pension,' said June. 'He calls it the dole.'

'Denial. They all do that.'

Dickie said, spitting scone, 'He took my telly.'

The television was back in its place when Dickie came in from the garden the next day. He plugged it in and switched it on and off, and then satisfied, went looking for June. She was in the lounge-room, checking the date stamps on her library books, sorting them into piles. Dickie started in on Craig, what the hell was the boy up to, where could he have got the dough from to get the TV out of hock, but June cut him off. 'It's back. That's the main thing.'

'But how? If he borrowed off a mate, he'll have to pay him back. So he'll have to pawn something else.'

June snapped a book shut. And suddenly Dickie understood. 'How much was it?'

She busied herself stuffing her books into a string bag. He waited.

'Thirty dollars.'

'Christ. Is that all he got?'

When Craig landed home after five days' walkabout, he was naked except for a strange pair of shorts that hung off his hips. He was nervy and his hair wild. His eyes cast about.

'God knows what's happened to his clothes,' June was telling the nurse on the phone.

Dickie looked in at Craig from the lounge-room doorway. He turned back to June. 'He's making those faces again.'

The nurse was over within the hour. She came out of Craig's room, looking grim, pressing the stud on her stiff leather bag. 'Boys are always worse at handling medication.'

Dickie straightened out the hose but still it didn't reach the mandarin tree. Be buggered how it could shrink up on him like that. He stuck the end of the hose in a bucket and bucketed water onto the fruit trees. It was a full day's job, the garden.

He was stacking some pruned branches out the front when a rusty old Toyota pulled up opposite and Craig got out the passenger side and a girl got out of the driver's seat. She slammed her door, and then opened it to slam it again. On the third slam the door shut tight.

Craig introduced the girl as Sharon. Sharon was wearing jeans, a belt with a big buckle and a tight, short-sleeved top. She looked sullenly at Dickie's old, torn gardening pants. How old was she? Twenty-one, twenty-two?

June had set up the tea things in the sun-room. So she'd known Sharon was coming all along. He might have changed his trousers, had she told him.

Sharon knocked back the tea and date loaf and asked for coffee. When she reached for the sugar, the sleeve rode up on her thin arm and Dickie saw the edge of her tattoo.

'You could have brought your little boy,' June was saying. 'There's plenty of space to play.'

Everyone turned to look through the glass doors at the deep backyard. Dickie thought, if kids were going to be coming round he'd have to put up a fence to stop them trampling on the vegies.

Craig, getting up, said he was going to cut Sharon some roses. Dickie watched him as he wandered about, snipping the best buds.

'What's your boy's name?' June in her stride now, finding out about children.

'Harley.'

'That's a nice name.' June would say that no matter what.

That made Sharon smile, the first smile they'd had out of her. 'My husband named him after his bike.'

'Do you think this is worth keeping?' Dickie asked.

'No, chuck it out.' Hunched forward with a tape measure around her neck, June fed a length of orange fabric through the machine. Crookedly, it appeared to Dickie.

'You haven't even looked at it.'

The machine stopped and June turned around. 'Oh, the cuckoo clock.'

'There's a whole box of clocks out there. Thought I might fix them up.'

'Well, if it keeps you off the streets.' June went back to her sewing.

A week after his shot, Craig arrived home with a new mate. The pair of them stood there on the footpath, and stared at the long line of stakes Dickie had laid out on the lawn and was painting in different colours.

'Going vampire-slaying, Grandad.'

'I guess I could. No, just using up bits of old paint. Those stakes'll last twenty years painted up like that.'

'How old are you now, Grandad?'

Dickie swirled his paintbrush in a jar of turps. He looked sideways at Craig's mate, who was wearing track pants and a grubby striped vest he must've been hot in.

'Grandad, this is Loco.'

Dickie shook his pudgy hand. 'Like the locomotive, eh?'

'Something like that.' Loco's spectacles were taped up at the corner.

'What happened to your specs?'

'I was climbing through a window.' Loco had a slow way of talking. 'And me glasses fell off and the arm broke off 'em.'

'What were you doing climbing through a window?'

'I was locked out.'

Dickie didn't pursue it. 'Come into the garage. I'll stick a bit of wire through the hinge.'

In the confined space of the garage, the smell of the boys' joggers was overwhelming. Dickie took some time shifting boxes to get at the cupboard that held bits of wire, and the boys meanwhile stared at his tools hanging along the wall in canvas pockets. Dickie said, poking through a shoebox, 'I think I'll just get this garage sorted out before I die.'

'You can't die, Grandad. You've got to outlast those stakes.'

When June suggested Craig help him down in the garden, Dickie doubted that he wanted Craig's help and that Craig would be interested, but he gave Craig an axe anyhow, a blunt one, and set him onto the monster Monstera. Craig did a bit of chopping without much enthusiasm, and then wandered round picking the ripe strawberries and eating them. Eventually he sat on the compost bin and rolled himself a cigarette.

'The Dutch hoe is a wonderful invention,' Dickie said, by way of conversation. He was dragging the hoe through the dirt, turning up garlic. 'Like digging up gold.' At the mention of gold, Craig got off the compost bin and came over to look, and then went back to his seat. Dickie felt the sun warm on his back through his shirt and singlet – a heartening sensation. He hammered in some of the newly painted stakes and began to tie up the tomatoes, using torn strips of June's old red skirt.

Craig said, 'I reckon I'll build myself a hut down here.'

Dickie stopped and straightened. Down where, exactly? On the vegetable patch? Or did he mean to chop down the fruit trees? But he said nothing and went back to tying up the tomatoes.

Later, when he was soaping his hands in the laundry tub, he said to June, 'I think Craig plans to stay with us a long time.'

Craig was in the toilet with the door open – the boy never shut himself in anywhere – when the cuckoo clock cuckooed six times. Dickie heard Craig burst out laughing, an echoey laugh around the tiles. Craig emerged, zipping up his fly, still laughing. 'What's with all these clocks, man?'

Dickie tore a slice of bread into his soup.

June, putting down her appointment book, was smiling too now.

'Clocks everywhere. What are you doing, Grandad? Timing yourself?'

Dickie spooned soup into his mouth. In fact, there was a clock now in every room – except Craig's. No point, the boy was timeless.

June said, 'Fixing things keeps your Grandad out of trouble.'

Craig and Loco were great mates. Every day now they borrowed June's Datsun, Loco driving. 'Buggers drive it till the tank's dry and then leave it for us to fill,' Dickie complained, but June didn't care. 'As long as it gets him out of the house. At least he's up early now.'

Before breakfast even, Craig would be ringing Loco. 'Hello, what have you been up to?'

'He just saw him yesterday,' Dickie said into his porridge.

The only condition June placed on the car-borrowing was that they didn't drive it to Sydney. 'I don't want you boys going up there buying drugs.'

'Who needs to go to Sydney, Nana? There are drugs all over Wollongong. You can buy drugs in this street.'

After they'd gone, June said, 'He's not backward in telling me stuff I'd rather not know.'

'Craig wants a hi-fi. He says he's going mad without music.'

'Going?' said Dickie.

June gave him a look. 'He bought two of these things yesterday.' She tapped two flat plastic containers on the bench. 'Something to do with laser.'

Dickie examined them. Pearl Jam. Pink Floyd. He saw the $29 sticker on one. 'Bought?'

'Well. He came home with them.'

The next evening, Dickie took Craig out to the garage. 'Got something to show you.' Building the mystery. Dickie rolled back the garage door and switched on the light. Craig stepped into the garage and stared.

'It used to be your mother's. Thought you could use it.'

Craig spun the turntable with his hand, and started to laugh.

Dickie's face fell. He'd spent all afternoon on the damn thing, cleaning the leads and the big speakers, oiling the turntable. He'd even tracked down a new stylus in one of the cupboards.

Craig had his head tipped back now, laughing. 'They don't make records any more, Grandad.'

Next cheque day, Craig landed home with a box labelled *Sony compact disc* and headed for his room. Dickie looked at June. 'Don't tell me he's swiped it.' Soon they heard music, creepy music Dickie thought, and an hour later Craig came out of his room, smiling drowsily.

'Must've been expensive,' said Dickie.

Craig picked through the bananas in the fruit bowl. Looking for the perfect one. Nothing but the best for Craig. 'No. I got it on time payment. If I keep up the instalments for four years, I get to keep it.'

'After you've paid for it three times over,' said Dickie.

'See. This is the sort of thing.' Dickie brought a packet of Bic shavers out of the bathroom to show the community nurse. There was only one shaver left in the packet. 'Usually when I buy these, they last me for oh, about six months, but Craig gets into them and he has to have a new one every time. It's not as though he's got a tough beard or anything.'

June said, 'We can't get petty.'

'Christ,' said Dickie. 'He spends more in a day than we do in a week.'

To the community nurse, who was calmly blowing her nose on her big hanky, Dickie added, 'I wake up at night thinking about him and I tell you, they are not pleasant thoughts.'

'At least now Craig is eating properly, sleeping properly,' June said.

'Eating and sleeping, alright. That's all he does. Eat, sleep, drink, smoke.' Dickie shifted his weight off his sore hip. 'And then there's that useless mate he hangs around with.'

'It's good he's got a mate.'

Dickie appealed to the nurse. 'It's killing me to be nice to him.'

Dickie woke suddenly on his back, heart thudding, feeling beached in the wash of moonlight. He listened but nothing moved in the house or outside, except a car taking the corner. Beside him, June was so still, she could have been dead.

Dickie got up to walk his hip a little and stopped at the window, lifting back the canvas blind. He saw the full moon riding high and the glossy leaves of the camellia turned silver – but in the driveway there was no car. So that's what had woken him.

Dickie sat on the bed, gently, careful not to wake June. Where would Craig be going at – he looked at his watch – three o'clock in the morning? On a hanger hooked over the swivel mirror, June's white bowling dress shone, palely, like the moon itself. His gaze rested there. That dress. Something of June inhabited its form, even when she wasn't wearing it.

In the morning the Datsun was back in place and Craig slept till the afternoon. Dickie said nothing to June. For some reason he wanted to protect her from that.

Dickie waited for Craig to go out. He opened Craig's door. The room was dark and potent with the smell of jogging shoes. He stepped inside, treading on a pile of clothes, and pulled the cord on the Venetian. Beside the rumpled bed, an ashtray spilled ash and butts onto the carpet. 'A pig's paddock,' Dickie muttered.

Dickie picked up the top book on a pile of dusty paperbacks. *Black Trillian. An epic fantasy of love and magic.* There was a letter inside, and recognising his daughter's writing on the envelope, he opened it up and began to read.

'You old snoop.'

June at the door. 'You should be ashamed, going through his things.'

'He goes through *ours*!'

But when June walked off, Dickie, chastened, put the letter back and after hunting out Craig's joggers to put through the wash, left, closing the door.

When Craig asked him one morning for five bucks for cigarettes, Dickie barked no. 'The boy should be paying board, not asking for money,' he told June.

'When he's really on top of things,' said June.

But then Dickie's blood pressure shot up suddenly, and when the doctor gave him pills and ordered rest, June drove him down to Bega, sitting close to the wheel, her dark lenses clipped down over her spectacles. All the way Dickie shifted in the car seat, trying to get his hip comfortable. June turned to look at him. 'You'll have to have it done.' The car swerved and Dickie said, 'Your driving's enough to make me.'

Yet the hotel bed was hard and Dickie slept badly, worrying what Craig was doing to the house, and after three days June drove him back to Wollongong.

All the blinds on the eastern side of the house were drawn. The kitchen stank of cigarettes and spirits. Pizza boxes sprawled across the bench. Three ashtrays overflowed onto the tablecloth. A hot plate was on, glowing red. Dickie went to switch it off and kicked over a stack of empty bottles. Jim Beam, every one of them. He grabbed a bottle by the neck as it rolled and, holding it up, said, 'How much does this stuff cost?'

In the lounge-room there was a box of Coco Pops and a stack of videos – *The Terminator*, *The Killing Fields*, *Dracula*. Fun viewing. At least the other rooms were untouched. Except, wouldn't you know it, the portable telly was gone again. Funny how it was always *his* telly.

June opened the dressing-table drawer and scratched about.

'Anything else gone?'

'No.'

'You sure?'

June nodded, sat down abruptly on the bed. She pushed up her glasses and pressed her thumb and forefinger into her closed eyes. 'A long drive,' she said.

Leaving June to rest, Dickie flattened and stacked the pizza boxes and put them in the recycle bin. Then he gathered up the empties and carried them out, and was about to dump them into the wheelie-bin, when he saw, lying at the bottom – a hypodermic needle. Dickie stared. He thought of HIV. He thought of June. Carefully he dropped the bottles inside, arranging them so that June wouldn't see the needle.

Dickie worked his knobby fingers into the pockets of Craig's clothes. No guilt this time. He found a condom, Sharon's address and number, scraps of old Tally Ho – and the pawn ticket. He held the ticket towards the light. *1 portable TV, 1 emerald cluster ring.* Emerald cluster ring?

Dickie was closing the wardrobe door when he saw the litter of plastic containers at the bottom of the wardrobe. He pushed back the clothes to get a better look. Six milk containers, the two-litre sort, each with a length of rubber hose inserted into the side. 'I'll be buggered,' he said. Gathering them all up by their handles, he carried them through to the kitchen where June was groping the groceries on the bench. 'I can't find my glasses.'

'See these?' said Dickie. 'Bongs, they're called. And look at this – *my* hose.'

June peered at the objects held up before her. 'He was always good at making things.'

Then Dickie showed her the pawn ticket. June held it up close and nodded.

'Why didn't you tell me? I gave you that ring.'

'Sometimes Dickie, things – possessions – just don't matter.'

Dickie took the phone into the study, closed the door and dialled Sharon's number.

Sharon was guarded. 'No, I haven't seen him. Not for a while.'

'We're worried. He's disappeared. He's been hitting the pot a bit lately.'

'The what? Oh.' He heard the smile in her voice. 'Well, Mr Shepherd, there isn't a drug in the world Craig hasn't tried.'

When Craig did finally come home, it was in a police car. The awkward young officer who brought him to the door said Craig had been found crying in the shopping mall, lost, unable to find his way out. Craig was bleary-eyed. His toenails were long and dirty. His hands shook when he tried to roll a cigarette.

The community nurse arrived clutching her stiff brown bag and went into Craig's room. Afterwards she consulted Dickie and June in the hall. 'He can't keep missing his shot. Each time he lets it go like that, the harder it is for him to climb back.'

'We don't want to put pressure on him,' said June, her voice quavering. 'Any pressure and he takes off. He did that with his mum and dad. Look – he's been kicked out by his uncle, his girlfriend, his friends. Even a squat. We're the end of the road. After us it's the street.'

'No. You can't push him. It's got to come from him.'

'He tries to get himself together, he really does.'

'Does he?' said Dickie.

'Schizophrenia robs you of your volition,' the nurse said calmly. 'It's the nature of the beast.'

When Craig was making sense again, Dickie decided to quiz him about the syringe in the bin. He waited for June to head off to a meeting with the mayor. First Craig denied any knowledge of it, he didn't use needles, ever, and then he said it was Loco's. 'He has morphine sometimes.'

'Then Loco can't stay here again. Or take the car at night. Is that clear?'

Craig nodded, his eyes sliding away.

Dickie tracked down the old key to his study and oiled the lock, and after shifting the portable TV and other things of value inside, kept the study locked.

'You walk round like a jailer with that great big key hanging off you,' said June.

'If I don't tie it to my belt, I'll lose it.'

'Like being in jail.'

'Well, when there's a thief in the house –'

'Don't say that. He's unwell.'

'So am I,' said Dickie.

And he told her that if she had any sense, she'd put her valuables in there too. Of course, she refused. But Dickie saw that even June was hiding her money and jewellery in her hanky drawer now.

Craig had been weeping for days. Moping round the house, not even bothering to ring Loco. June took him out for a coffee, and later summarised for Dickie – 'Sharon's dumped him. He's depressed. He's got no love interest now.'

'No sex, you mean.'

'Oh you cynic.'

Two weeks later, Craig up and moved his things into the laundry. He slept on a camp-bed there and set out his CD player on the ironing board. The move seemed to inspire him. He talked about getting the laundry extended. He could do it himself even, just move the wall out another two, three metres. That way he could get a couch in, and a fridge. And a shower in the corner. Maybe a phone. Like a flatette.

Dickie, sitting on the back porch, said to June, 'I mean, where does he think you're going to do the washing?'

Craig had a TAFE handbook by his laundry bunk for a week before he announced he'd picked out a course. June and Dickie pressed together, peering at the circled item.

Dickie snorted. 'That's a good one. Explosives.'

June was arguing with someone up on the back porch. Dickie struck his spade into the earth so it stood upright and went out under the vines. On the porch, a young man in a purple suit and dark glasses with his hair slicked back chewed languidly, his hands in his trouser pockets. Dickie went up the path towards them, stamping his boots to shake the dirt.

'You lot prey on people like him.' June's head jutted forward. 'People too poor or too silly to pay outright.'

The man stopped chewing. He looked in Dickie's direction. Behind him, an old gent in shorts and filthy singlet carried Craig's CD out of the laundry. The man in the suit followed the old gent down the steps. June stood at the top of the driveway and stared after them.

Dickie pressed his foot to the floor of the car – June, beside him, was driving too fast for this potholed road. Craig in the back seat was silent. His idea to come up here, to the Hawkesbury, looking for peace. Peace and *work*, Dickie hoped he realised.

The Krishna who greeted them spoke so softly Dickie could hardly hear him. He could smell him, though – Indian oils, or was it incense? The fellow suggested that June and Dickie take a look around, which they did, tramping in the dusty heat, nodding in embarrassed friendliness at anyone they ran into. When his hip became sore, Dickie rested and watched a group of orange-robed women teaching toddlers a song in the shade of an angophora. Regressive for women, he would have thought, this religion.

When they returned to the car, Craig and the Krishna were waiting.

'Craig's going to stay a few nights,' the Krishna said softly. Dickie turned his good ear towards him. 'But we've agreed that he's not suited to living here on a permanent basis. I think he needs more care than we can give.'

Dickie nodded. Psychiatric.

Craig's face puckered. He looked away, squinting at the women in the distance. June gave him a hug and Dickie patted him awkwardly, before they got back in the dusty Datsun.

'You'd think they'd want a new convert,' June said as the car jerked forward, spraying stones.

Dickie watched Craig receding in the side mirror; Craig in clean jeans, picking up his zippered bag, eager yet forlorn. This morning, getting into the car, Craig had said to him, *I don't want to be mad.*

'It shows they've got sense.'

'How?' June slapped down the sun visor.

'Well, if something happened, it'd bring bad publicity. The last thing they want.'

'If something happened. Like what?'

He didn't answer and June turned her head fully toward him. 'Like what, Dickie?'

Another moonlit night and Dickie in bed heard the car backing down the drive. He got up and saw, as the Datsun swung out and braked, the shapes of Loco at the wheel and Craig beside him. Then the headlights flicked on, the car shot forward and the boys were gone.

Early next morning in the dewy cold, Dickie checked the car and found a ding in the mud-spattered rear panel. All the car doors were unlocked. He opened the passenger door and felt under the seat for a rag. What he felt was something hard and cold, a metal object. A *crowbar*. His hand patted round, distinguishing more tools. He pulled them out. *His* wire cutters, *his* screwdriver, and the unfamiliar crowbar. Dickie sat down heavily in the passenger seat, one leg in, one leg out, and stared at the tools beneath his right foot. What had those stupid boys been up to? He thought of Craig's terror of police, of confinement. Christ, if they locked him up, that'd be the end of him.

'Is something wrong?' June had come out onto the driveway. She looked frail in her nightie, the form of her breasts hanging low at her waist. He stuck his head out. 'No, just hunting down a spanner. I'm coming in now.'

When June had gone back inside, Dickie heaved himself out of the seat and gathered up the tools. He went down to the back garden and, screened by the vines, began to dig. Beneath the topsoil, the earth was clayey and the digging heavy-going. He tied a strip of cloth round his forehead to stop the sweat stinging his eyes. When he'd finished, he strewed leaf mulch over the top. He emerged from the garden the same time as Craig entered through the side gate. Craig was barefoot and Dickie caught a whiff of pot even from where he stood, watching. If I say something about the tools, Dickie thought, he will piss off – *and bang goes the medication.*

Craig jumped when he saw Dickie and his eyes opened wildly. 'Fuck, Grandad. Killing Fields.'

June was animated as she stood there on the lawn, in her pink belted dress and burgundy heels, telling him the story:

'I took him through the hospital and I said – Look, empty beds, empty beds, and then I took him into the psych wing and of course, every one of them was occupied. All bad cases too. The whole ward's full, I said to Bob. If there's a psychiatric emergency tonight, they'll have to turn them away. And Bob gets all excited and says – Yes! Something must be done! And so I said, But as well as the beds – I thought strike while the iron's hot, how often have I tried to tell him this before – As well as the beds, we need a crisis team. At least ten people. And Bob was somehow really caught up in it and he said, Consider it done! And in front of everyone, he kisses me on the cheek and says, That's from Bob Macleay, Lord Mayor. Then he goes off and comes back and kisses me again, on the other cheek, and says, And that's from Bob Macleay, Member of Parliament, then he goes off and comes back – should've been in the theatre, that bloke – and this time he kisses me on the mouth, in front of everyone, and says, And that's from Bob Macleay, the man.'

Dickie kneaded his hip with the heel of his hand. What did the mayor think he was doing kissing his wife? Bloody showman. 'Well, we'll see what comes of it.' The shine went out of June's face and he added, 'Sounds promising though.'

June looked down at Dickie's hand. 'Can't keep putting it off.'

'There's an article today, as a matter of fact. It says there's a ten per cent failure or death rate on the hip replacement.'

June put her hand on his shoulder.

Then the side gate rattled and they both turned to see two police officers, a man and a woman. Dickie's heart gave a thump.

'We tried the front door,' said the policewoman. She had a Slavic accent. The male officer manipulated the catch on the gate and they came into the yard. June walked slowly towards them, her heels sinking into the grass. With difficulty, Dickie pushed himself off the wooden seat.

The policewoman said, 'We are looking for Craig Petrovic.' The way she said Pet-*ro*-vic sounded authentic, and ominous somehow. Beside her, the male cop scanned the yard.

'We haven't seen him for days,' said June faintly.

'Since Thursday,' put in Dickie, as he tried to remember exactly when it was. He felt a pain jamming his hip and longed to walk up and down.

The policewoman asked about Craig's friends, and then said, 'Is that your vehicle in the drive?'

'Yes,' said June.

The policewoman gave nothing away, simply instructed them to have Craig ring the police station as soon as he came home.

After the gate had snapped to, and the squeak of police boots faded, June and Dickie stared at each other, wonderingly.

When Dickie came out one morning and saw that every rose in the garden had gone, he nodded. So that's where Craig was. Without telling June, Dickie caught a train to Woonoona and walked down to the conglomerate of Housing Commission flats near the beach. He found Number Twelve and pressed the buzzer. The bolt shot back on the door and then Sharon behind the wire door said, oh hello, wary and surprised, before going to fetch a key.

'Sorry, I have to keep it locked.' The key clicked and she held the screen door open for him. 'We're all solo mums down here and every lout about the place knows it.'

Tinny-sounding music played from a radio on a small cane table. A boy of about three was pushing a toy motor bike round the skirting board. The boy was neatly dressed and the flat clean – she was obviously trying.

Sharon gestured for him to sit on the cushioned cane sofa but she herself remained standing with her arms hugging her midriff. Today she was wearing a singlet top and the rose tattoo on her arm was clearly visible.

Dickie said, 'About Craig –' He saw in the kitchen the vase full of roses, now starting to droop.

'It's finished.'

'I know. We're worried –'

'Look, Mr Shepherd, I had to kick him out again. I know he's feeling down but . . .' Her chest swelled with a long breath. 'I want a job and a flat somewhere else by the time Harley hits school. And I'm doing a hospitality course at TAFE this year.'

Hospitality. They all did that.

'Craig's a liability. The sort of person who drags you down.' Her voice was getting high and thin. 'I need a responsible partner. I know, with a kid and everything, that sounds like I'm asking a lot.'

'No. You deserve a lot.'

Her face softened. She went on less defensively, 'Craig can be very sweet and romantic and all that, and he's fun to be with, but . . .'

Dickie nodded. Personally he wouldn't wish Craig on any girl. He said, 'He's nicked off. I need to find him.'

She was silent.

'Before the cops do.'

'Oh.' Willing now to help, suggesting a few places. 'Or you could try the Charles. He hangs there a bit. Him and Loco.'

When Dickie left, walking back up the short path, he heard the key turn in the screen door and the bolt slide. He looked at the identical flats around him. How stupid, putting all the single mothers in one block.

A Saturday night and the Charles was noisy. In the haze it seemed to Dickie that everyone was smoking. He hobbled between the pool tables. He had walked here and his hip was nagging him. Coming into this place put Dickie in mind of the time, as a young surveyor in a new town, he'd stumbled into a shearer's pub on a Saturday afternoon – except back then it had been the other way round, and the timidity he'd felt in the face of all that brawn was on account of his youth.

A big bloke lining up a shot, stepped back and trod on Dickie's foot. The bloke apologised loudly and banged him on the back. Dickie had a feeling the whole world was young and rough and he didn't belong in it.

He was passing from the first bar into the back bar when he glimpsed the pudgy figure of Loco disappearing through the end door. At least it'd looked like Loco's vest, the grubby striped one, and Dickie started on through the bar. An under-aged girl walking slowly, steering three schooners, got in the way, and by the time Dickie reached the door, Loco wasn't in sight.

Instead, in the car park, a skinny bare-chested youth was swinging a broken bottle at two long-haired fellows, while a girl in black screamed, pulling his arm, her boots crunching in the puddle of broken glass.

And through the exit on the far side of the car park, a pair of tail lights dipped.

Dickie went round to the drive-in bottle shop and told the hefty man at the till, 'Blokes trying to kill each other out there.'

The man, reaching for the phone, said, 'So what's new.'

Craig had been gone a month, and this night Dickie and June found themselves up having a glass of port at three in the morning, talking about Craig, back and forth, the same old stuff.

June said, 'I hope he gets hospitalised. It's his only hope.'

The police had come round yet another time and June had gone to great lengths to explain about Craig's condition. 'On deaf ears,' she'd said later.

Dickie looked at her, saw the darkness of insomnia around her eyes.

'You know the last time he was in hospital,' she said, 'they found heroin in his urine.'

Dickie stared. No, he didn't know.

Then one sunny afternoon when Dickie was napping alongside June in the easy chairs in the sun-room, he woke, startled, with June squeezing his knee. She had her finger to her lips. Dickie listened. He heard a coal truck rumble by on the distant highway – and then a scratching sound, in their bedroom. Quietly, he and June made their way down the hall and peered in the doorway.

It was Craig, dressed like a swaggie, riffling through June's hanky drawer. He'd pulled the drawer right out and set it on the bed. When he saw them, he started wildly. 'I was looking for a hanky, Nana,' he said and plucked out a handkerchief, a white lace one. He mumbled about being depressed and sniffed into the hanky, pretending to cry.

Dickie stared, appalled. His blood thudded. He could plainly see the wad of twenties in Craig's hand. And now June was sobbing and Dickie knew it wasn't for the money or the things in the drawer. It was for their grandson, reduced to this elaborate sham, lying to his grandparents, acting, not knowing where the acting stopped, not knowing what were lies anyhow.

'I hate it,' Craig was saying now, and he was actually crying this time, the tears spilling down his face, hanging from his nose. And in his confusion, he was dropping money and grabbing at hankies.

And suddenly Dickie's anger dwindled and he felt a wash of sad love for the boy. For June was right – Craig was mad, not bad, and getting madder. And Dickie feared for his grandson, feared for what would become of him, as he'd never feared before.

Contributors

Garry Disher grew up on a farm in the mid-north of South Australia, the setting for *Manhunt* and his latest novel, *The Sunken Road*. A full-time writer for many years, he is the author of novels, short story collections, the Wyatt thrillers and award-winning books for children.

Ann Dombroski grew up in Wollongong and has travelled extensively, working in Greece and Spain. Her short stories have appeared in a wide range of journals and magazines.

Allan Donald left school at the age of fourteen and has worked as an orderly in a psychiatric hospital, a cane-cutter, a gardener and a dump attendant. He lives in the Northern Territory.

Fiona McGregor was born and bred in Sydney. She is the author of a novel, *Au Pair*, and a collection of interlinked short stories, *Suck My Toes*, winner of the Steele Rudd Award in 1995.

James McQueen was born in Tasmania and has worked as a factory hand, fruit-picker, truck-driver, ship's cook, weather observer and window dresser. He is the author of six novels, including *Hook's Mountain* and *White Light*, and his short stories have won a number of national and international awards. He lives with his second wife in north-eastern Tasmania.

Gillian Mears was born in New South Wales in 1964 and lives near the town of Grafton. Her works include *Fine Flour* and *The Mint Lawn* which won the *Australian/*

Vogel Literary Award. Her most recent book is *The Grass Sister*.

Les Murray grew up on a dairy farm at Bunyah on the north coast of New South Wales and became a full-time writer in 1971. Winner of the Petrarch Prize, his poetry has been highly praised throughout the English-speaking world.

Zyta Plavic left home at sixteen and has lived in various towns along the New South Wales central coast. She is currently serving a nine-year prison sentence for conspiracy to import 350 grams of heroin. She was refused Legal Aid funding for an appeal, and is attempting to appeal on her own.

Margaret Simons grew up in South Australia and has worked as a journalist. Her first novel, *The Ruthless Garden*, won the inaugural Angus & Robertson Bookworld Prize and her second novel, *The Truth Teller*, is to be published in mid-1996.

Leonie Stevens was born during the Cuban missile crisis and grew up in Melbourne. Her interests include art, film, sex, television and eating eggplant. She is co-director of *Scram* art collective, and her first novel, *Nature Strip*, was published in 1994.

Archie Weller was born in Subiaco, Western Australia, in 1957. His first novel, *Day of the Dog*, was adapted as a feature film and his collection of short stories, *Going Home*, received wide critical praise.